The Cinderella Princess

The Cinderella Princess

A Royal Holiday Romance

Melissa McClone

TULE
PUBLISHING

Dedication

For everyone who hangs out with me at my Facebook page. Thanks for your friendship and support. You're the best!

An extra shout out to: Andra D, Mary D, Denise H, Christine J, Alayne L, Barb M, Heidi P, Connie R, Janine R, Eileen W, Ranee W, and Kenderly W!

Thanks for your help brainstorming names of countries!

Acknowledgments

Special thanks to Holiday Books and Senior Editor Kelly Hunter for including me in the Royal Holiday series with Madeline Ash, Jeannie Moon and Kathleen O'Brien!

Chapter One

EMILY RODGERS SAT in the backseat of a rusted-out taxi next to her longtime friend and pseudo-assistant, Addie Cahill. The ad agency should have had a limousine waiting at the airport, not an old cab that burped and passed gas. But Emily had been sent to Alvernia, a small European country, for damage control, not a holiday.

The taxi driver zigzagged around two cyclists.

Her head ached and her body longed for sleep after four flights and fifteen sleepless hours of travel from San Diego, California, but she found herself captivated by the postcard perfect street lined with charming shops and cafés. Elaborate engraved wooden signs hung from each storefront. People filled the sidewalks, enjoying the sunny spring day.

She rested her head against the hard backseat. The ibuprofen she'd taken at the airport hadn't kicked in yet. "I hope it's not too far to the hotel."

"Shouldn't be." Concern clouded Addie's eyes. "Have a

plan?"

"Yes." Not one hundred percent set, but Emily would figure out the other details soon.

So what if she worked in advertising not television? Her boss, Don Peabody, wanted his wife Kendra's production company to succeed. He was willing to use whatever resources necessary, including Emily, to make that happen. This wasn't the first time she'd been forced to help a fledgling reality TV show. If she received an overdue promotion, she hoped this one would be the last.

"Once I save the day again, they'll have no choice but to make me a partner."

"You deserve it and a raise, too."

Emily nodded. She should have been promoted last summer, but her boss told her that she needed to bring in a top level client first. She'd been working on doing that ever since.

The taxi jerked to a stop. The driver swore. A translation guide wasn't necessary. "Traffic jam."

An imaginary clock went tick-tock in her mind. She pressed her lips together to keep from saying anything. The cars on the road weren't the driver's fault.

She checked her cellphone. Nearly one o'clock in the afternoon. Traveling made her lose all sense of time. She stretched her arms over her head and yawned.

"I see the hotel." Leaning forward, Addie's long, brown ponytail swung back and forth like a pendulum. "A crowd is gathered out front."

Emily did a double take, noticed cameras. Lots of them.

Not just people. Paparazzi. They jockeyed for position like hungry piranhas hunting for their next victim.

Every muscle twisted into a going-to-need-a-massage bundle of knots.

Only one person could cause a near riot in the quaint, picturesque town surrounded by snowcapped peaks—His Royal Highness Lucas Alexander Leopold Casimir von Rexburg. The reason she'd been sent here. Black sheep and reckless royal didn't begin to describe King Leopold's youngest son, who was so far down the line of succession he wasn't considered a spare heir, but a liability.

Emily's French-manicured fingernails dug into the car door's armrest. "I'm going to kill him."

"That's what Nick said he wanted do, too."

Nick Cahill was Addie's husband, a former Green Beret hired by Emily to handle security during the filming of a new reality TV show called *The Search for Cinderella* starring Prince Luc as he looked for a princess to marry.

"Nick couldn't believe the prince ran off while everyone was suffering food poisoning," Addie said.

Based on Luc's reputation, Emily could believe it. She tapped her finger against her face. She was here to get the filming and dating back on track after the producer fired their royalty consultant. She had five days to fix the problems before she returned to San Diego for a client presentation.

The biggest obstacle to her succeeding was the prince himself. A plan formed in Emily's mind. "With Nick's special ops training, I bet he can dispose of a body and leave no evidence."

Addie drew back, a frown on her pretty face. "Stop. Now."

"Okay, maybe death's a bit extreme." And no doubt would be a PR nightmare. But there had to be something they—okay, Nick—could do so Prince Luc would have to be replaced. Any other handsome royal would have found a fiancée and be making wedding plans by now. "Maiming might be covered by insurance."

"Innocent until proven guilty."

Emily remembered the photos that had gone viral after the prince's strip poker game with college women on tour with an a cappella choir. The next day, she'd hired Nick to babysit the royal rogue. That had been a month ago.

"There's nothing innocent about Prince Luc." His name tasted bitter. Emily wished she hadn't thrown away her water bottle at the airport. "The man is the devil in disguise."

Addie tsked. "How can you say that? You've never met him."

"True." Hearing about his exploits was bad enough. "But he's living up to his reputation of being a self-entitled, spoiled twit."

"Tell your boss he needs to be fired."

"I did when problems started the first week of filming,

but no one listened. The production company believes the show will be a hit, and they're brainstorming a royal wedding spinoff."

"Has the prince found a bride?"

"No." And if something didn't change soon, the show would have to be retitled *How To Lose a Princess in 10 Hours or Less*. Not one princess was interested in a second date with Prince Luc. Few agreed to a first one. The majority wanted nothing to do with the guy. "But I have the names of nobility from duchesses to baronesses to add to the list of princesses."

"Why not a commoner?" Addie asked. "That worked out well for Prince William."

"King Leopold wants his son to marry a royal. That was a requirement for the show."

The cab backfired. Emily's heart pounded. A good thing they were almost at the hotel.

Addie's lips twisted. "What about love?"

Her words held a touch of whimsy. Not surprising. She believed in happily ever after and one true love.

Emily knew better thanks to her divorced parents. Being with a man could be enjoyable. Everyone needed companionship and attention at times. Affection, too. But forget about making things permanent.

"It's reality TV," Emily said. "No one cares about love."

"I did. Nick, too."

"The two of you are in love." Last June, Emily had cast

Addie and Nick in a reality TV show and ended up with a hit show. "The prince's father ordered Luc to go on the show and find a bride. He's only doing his duty."

"How sad."

Emily shrugged. "That's the life of a royal."

"Maybe that's why the prince is so…troubled."

Troubled? Yeah, right. More like a troublemaker.

"No one is forcing Luc to hang around half-naked women and drink until he passes out." Thankfully the photos of the prince's party habits had stopped being uploaded to social media once Nick arrived on the set.

"I read about the fabulous events Prince Luc puts on to raise money for his charity foundation," Addie said. "At least he's trying to do good."

Trying wasn't enough. The fundraisers were probably excuses to have a good time. His just-have-fun party attitude made finding him a wife impossible. "I wish he'd *be* good for once."

The cab double-parked twenty feet away from the hotel.

"This is as close as I can park." The driver spoke English with a slight accent. "You'll have to get out here."

"Fine." Emily paid him. "We can handle our own luggage."

The driver removed their suitcases from the trunk and carried the bags to the sidewalk.

The sun shone bright in a clear blue sky. Emily squinted, then put on her sunglasses. The temperature was pleasant, only a slight breeze. The mountain air refreshed her after breathing in the recirculated air in the various planes.

She grabbed the handle of her suitcase. "Ready?"

"Yes." Addie wore sunglasses and a San Diego Padres cap. She held the handle of her wheeled bag. "But will the prince be ready for us?"

Emily pulled her luggage. "He'd better be."

A man ran past, bumping into her. She stumbled forward. The pavement rose to greet her.

Addie grabbed Emily's arm and kept her upright. "Hey, you jerk."

The man, who carried a camera bag, kept going. Typical.

"No worries." Emily smoothed her tunic over her pants then picked up her suitcase by the extended handle. Probably shouldn't have worn new shoes. They felt tight after the flight. "He's only thinking about a celebrity being in the vicinity."

Him and two dozen others.

Chaotic was the only way to describe the crowd in front.

Prince Luc's location and the show were supposed to be top secret. That was one reason they weren't filming in Alvernia until the end. The king's youngest son drew attention wherever he went.

"If I pinch myself, do you think I'll wake up and discover I'm having a bad dream?" she asked Addie.

"This might be your nightmare, but I've been dreaming about seeing Nick."

Emily shook her head. "Newlyweds."

"Don't knock marriage until you try it."

She didn't want a boyfriend let alone a husband. Casual dates when she felt lonely were good enough for now. She needed to focus on her career.

"Let's see if you're singing the same tune after your one year anniversary." Emily continued toward the hotel. "I'm not in any rush to take that plunge."

"Not every man is like your dad."

Logically, Emily knew that. Convincing her heart would take some doing. She squeezed past the throngs of paparazzi. Finally she reached the uniformed doorman.

"I'm Emily Rodgers." She removed her sunglasses to look the man in the eyes. "I have a reservation."

He opened the door. "Please check in at the front desk."

"Thank you." She stepped inside. Addie followed.

Cool air greeted Emily. The scent of money, too. Plush carpeting and heavy gold drapes swallowed the noise from the crowd outside. Old World was the only way to describe the décor with hanging chandeliers, gilded wood molding and exquisite oil paintings on display. The luxurious atmosphere seemed one-hundred-and-eighty degrees from the party animal prince who would be more comfortable at a college fraternity house.

At the front desk, she handed an envelope full of cash to a man behind the counter. Inside was the amount Nick had told her to pay. "I'm Emily Rodgers."

"We've been expecting you." The man handed her a room card. "You'll find what you're looking for in Suite 428. Will you need anything else?"

"Send up Nick Cahill when he arrives."

The man replied with a nod.

A few minutes later, Emily stood in front of Suite 428. A *Do Not Disturb* sign hung on the door handle. Was the prince alone? Or would they be disturbing a romantic rendezvous?

Addie stared down the hallway toward the elevator. "We've never met the prince. He might not take kindly to us bursting into his room."

"Luc chose to disappear like a rebellious teenager. Now he has to face the consequences."

Those included Emily. She knocked.

No answer.

She slid the card into the door reader. The little diode next to the card slot turned green. She turned the handle.

Addie sighed. "I hope you know what you're doing."

"No worries."

Emily might not have a firm plan in mind, but she did her best thinking under pressure. So what if the guy was royalty? A random accident of birth didn't make him different or special.

She pushed open the door.

Darkness greeted her. No movement or sounds, either.

"Is he gone?" Addie whispered.

"Let's find out."

Emily turned on the nearest light switch. She saw a sitting area, decorated in white and gold.

Someone grunted. Not a passionate moan, but an I'm-not-feeling-well groan.

Addie sucked in a breath. "I have a bad feeling about this."

So did Emily, but she chalked up the thought to jet lag. She could handle anything. That was why she'd been sent. "Come on. Let's go meet our runaway prince."

LIGHT HIT PRINCE Lucas Alexander Leopold Casimir von Rexburg's eyes like an unexpected camera flash. Spots appeared. A jagged pain zigzagged through his head. Covering his face with his hands, he swore.

"I only speak English, Your Highness," an unfamiliar feminine voice said.

"Turn off the damn light," Luc repeated in English.

"I can switch off the lamp, but it's time to get up, sir."

Each word hammered at his foggy, needs-more-sleep brain. He needed rest, not conversation. Darkness, not light.

"The paparazzi are downstairs," she continued.

Damn. They'd found him. But he'd escaped the hoard with cameras before. This time would be no different.

"I'll sleep for another hour or so, then I can leave through a service entrance."

He'd partied late into the night in the hotel's VIP lounge. He didn't remember bringing a woman back to his hotel room, or if this was even his room. But why else would she be with him?

He rolled over and buried his face into a pillow. The darkness was a welcome relief. Now to return to sleep…

"You need to wake up." The woman spoke with a sense of urgency. She'd dropped the *sir*, a breach of etiquette since he hadn't given her permission. Unless he'd done so last night. "I can't do this without you."

She meant sex. He must be on familiar terms with her. A smile tugged at his lips. Waking up might not be so bad. He'd fall asleep faster after they'd finished.

He turned his head toward the sound of her voice. Blinked open his eyes. Cringed at the chainsaw slicing his brain in half. Squeezed his eyelids together.

That didn't help.

Bloody hell, how much had he drunk?

"Wake up."

She sounded annoyed, perhaps angry. Luc must have fallen asleep last night. Disappointed her. Steeling himself for the onslaught of pain, he opened his eyes. Somehow he managed not to cringe or moan.

"Forgive me, *ma cherie*."

A blurry, unrecognizable figure dressed in black stood next to the bed. He blinked, until his vision sharpened. Straight, blonde hair fell to her shoulders in a stylish, practical cut. Attractive, possibly pretty if she stopped frowning and smiled.

"I did not mean to ignore you by sleeping the day away." He ignored the woodpecker chipping at his brain. "Get undressed, come back to bed and I shall make it up to you. Ten-fold."

Sharp green eyes—the color of the emeralds in his mother's tiara—collided with his gaze. "The royal scepter appears to be in working order in spite of the amount of alcohol you drank."

Royal scepter? He glanced down. A white sheet covered his naked body, but didn't hide the fact that he was hard. Damn.

She wasn't acting embarrassed so he wouldn't, either.

"Not any alcohol. Champagne. The drink of royalty. And lovers," Luc added for effect. "I can order a bottle of *Bollinger* if you'd like. Unless you'd prefer something else. Your wish is my command."

The woman looked at him like he was a criminal, guilty of whatever crime she believed he'd committed. "I'm not a royal groupie."

"Never thought you were." A woman who wanted to seduce or be seduced by a prince would never button her shirt to her neck. This one was dressed for a business meeting or a funeral service. "Who are you?"

"Emily Rodgers."

He didn't know the name, but he'd heard names, hundreds of names, thousands of names. Ones he rarely remembered. Why should he care what she was called unless she planned on undressing and getting into his bed?

"I just arrived," she continued. "I was sent to help you. Not have sex with you."

That explained her outfit and her tone. Not to mention her presence in his hotel room. "Are you alone?"

"My assistant is getting you a glass of water."

He tried to ignore the lightning bolt pain in his head. "Who sent you?"

"Don Peabody."

Peabody-Franks was the US advertising firm associated with the reality TV show's production company, but his father could still be the puppet master behind this farce of finding a princess bride.

A noise sounded in the bathroom. Something clattered against the floor. Water ran. Must be the assistant.

Luc wanted to get up, move, but he didn't see any clothing nearby. Had the hotel management put him to bed last night? "Tell me how you plan to help me."

"First we go back to Italy to film." A smile still hadn't cracked her tight lips. "I brought a list of additional bride candidates since the others haven't…worked out."

"Not my fault. I'm doing what I can."

"Really?" She motioned to him lying in bed. "Running away and overindulging in champagne isn't helping. Princesses are turning down first dates with you. We need one that will at least go out with you once if we're ever going to find a woman to accept your marriage proposal."

Each word slapped his face. The sting, however, was nothing new. "If you're trying to make me feel worse, you're succeeding."

"That wasn't my intention." Her voice softened slightly. Her expression didn't. "But sugarcoating your situation isn't going to find you a bride."

"I appreciate your honesty." Few told him the truth. Others only repeated what his father wanted said.

Birth order had determined Luc's fate long before he was born. Being the youngest child of the king meant no one had expectations he'd amount to much. Unlike his six older siblings, he'd had few rules to follow growing up. Spoiled, yes. Indulged, all the time, especially by his mother. That was why he hadn't thought his parents would pressure him to marry like the others.

"I do need to find a wife," Luc admitted. "But I don't understand how you're supposed to help me unless you know of a princess living in a tower with no electricity or a noblewoman who's run out of other marriage options."

"I don't know any women like that, but trust me. I'll be able to help you."

"Are you a matchmaker?"

"I'm an account executive at the advertising agency."

That didn't tell him much, but he hoped she wasn't like the worthless royalty consultant hired by the production crew. "Tell me the difference between a marchioness or a viscountess."

"I have no idea, but I'm happy to find out."

Not a bad answer. "That's more than the show's former royalty expert offered to do."

"I'll do whatever has to be done for the show to be a hit."

Her confidence appealed to him. "A true professional."

Defiance flashed in her eyes. "Is there any other kind?"

Her ballsy tone impressed him. He guessed she succeeded, more than she failed. Maybe she would be the right person to help him find a bride. "The hotel allowed you into my room…"

"Nick spoke to them."

Of course, who else? The man had ruined many an opportunity for fun since he arrived a month ago. But Luc had one more thing to do before leaving the country. No one would stop him.

Another woman approached the bed. She wore a baseball cap and carried a glass of water. A smile lit up her beautiful face.

Smiling hurt from his teeth to his brain, but Luc did his best. He wanted to make a better impression on this one. "Hello there. You must be the assistant."

"I am." She handed him the glass and two white pills. "These should help you feel better, Your Highness."

"Thank you." This was the kind of care Luc was used to. He took the pills and downed the entire glass of water.

Refreshing and needed. Both the liquid and the woman. "There's no need for formality. Please call me Luc."

"I'm Addie."

"Nice to meet you, Addie."

Something landed on his midsection—the thick, white robe provided by the hotel.

"What?" he asked.

The woman in black—he'd forgotten her name—glared at him. Forget shooting daggers. She was firing RPGs.

"Addie is my assistant. She's also Nick Cahill's wife. Unless you'd prefer to be known as Princess Lucy in the future, you'd better watch yourself around her. If you're not wearing anything under the sheet, put on the robe before Nick arrives."

Luc was naked. The bodyguard with hawk-like vision had never made him feel safer or more imprisoned at the same time. No doubt the man would be overprotective of his wife.

"I'll refill your water." Addie picked up the glass and walked away.

Luc would put on the robe with her out of the room. He also wanted to see how Miss Prim-and-Proper Professional handled the unexpected. Maybe he could get her to loosen up and smile. "I'll put on the robe now."

He moved the robe to the side and threw back the sheet.

Her eyes widened. Her lips parted. Her gaze lingered longer on his naked body than he expected.

Interesting. He'd thought she would gasp, turn around, act upset. Not…look at him.

She blinked, raised her gaze to meet his. "I don't know what you're trying to do, but I'm not impressed."

"Perhaps not, but you are blushing."

Her hand flew to her cheek. "I'm not."

Luc liked that she hadn't been sure and checked. Not one hundred percent in control. He wondered how else he could get her to react. "Only a touch of pink."

She pressed her lips together. "Put on the robe."

The woman ground out each word. Not one hundred percent professional. Perhaps attracted, in spite of her words.

Mission accomplished. He sat.

The room tilted, spun. He clutched the bottom sheet. Didn't help. His stomach flipped upside down.

"You're turning green," she said. "Here's a trash can."

Luc closed his eyes. That helped. Sort of. He felt as if he were spinning.

"It's going to be okay." Her tone was compassionate and warm, not businesslike. Could she have developed a heart in the last fifteen seconds? What was her name? Em…?

"I can do this." Keeping his eyes closed, he tugged on the robe. The terry cloth fabric felt like sandpaper against his skin. His fingers fumbled with the belt. He sucked in a breath. Wished his stomach would stop churning like a whirlpool. "I need a shower."

That would make him feel better.

Luc swung his legs over the edge of the bed, then stood.

The room tilted to his left. He reached out, grabbed hold of Em-something and tumbled to the bed, landing on top of her.

His chest pressed against her soft breasts. His face was inches from hers. Her green eyes widened. Her lips, soft and pink, parted.

Forget about a hangover. Heat rushed through him. The urge to kiss her was strong. Such nice lips. Add a little color…

She pushed against his chest. "What the hell? I'm not some princess-wannabe turned on by Alvernia's version of Adonis."

Luc considered her words. There was enough of a compliment in them to make him hesitate. "Adonis? Like what you see?"

She cringed. "No."

The one word spoke volumes.

Luc rolled to the side, then sat on the edge of the bed. The room kept spinning. Putting his head between his knees might be prudent. He stared at the carpet.

She moved away from him. "You're still wasted."

No, he was naked and reliant on a woman he'd only met with a name he couldn't remember. Said woman also turned him on, even with his head about to implode. Strange. The assistant was more his type, but this one intrigued him.

"I'm hungover. Not drunk," Luc announced in the royal

voice he'd perfected over the years. She'd surprised him. His turn to see what else she could handle. "I'm going to need your help taking a shower."

Chapter Two

HELP HIM SHOWER? No way. Emily needed to settle her sprinting pulse and stop her body from buzzing with awareness over this blue-blooded player who didn't mind exposing himself to, well, her.

His mussed, I'm-too-sexy wavy brown hair brushed his shoulders. Pale skin tone—a result of his hangover?—didn't detract from the high cheekbones, straight nose and full lips. Classically handsome described him. His only physical flaw seemed to be a small scar beneath his left eye. But the slight imperfection made his looks more interesting.

From an accident, sports or a fight? Most likely a jealous boyfriend or husband. Yeah, she could see that.

Emily realized she was staring and looked away. She focused on artwork hanging on the wall. A gilded framed oil painting. The landscape consisting of rich, jewel-tone colors fit the luxurious décor of the room and Prince Luc himself.

She'd known he was handsome from his photographs,

but she hadn't been prepared for his knock-her-down charisma and sex appeal. Or the sound of his voice that washed over her like a caress. Or him wearing nothing, but a smile.

She took a breath, then another. She still felt like she'd sprinted a hundred yard dash and needed a breather.

Addie returned with a full glass of water. Her gaze traveled from the prince to Emily. "Everything okay in here?"

"Fine." Luc took the water and drank.

Maybe he was fine. Emily wasn't. She took two steps back.

Had she really called him Alvernia's Adonis?

So not good.

But the guy did have a killer body…face…blue eyes… Those thick eyelashes were to-die-for. Seriously.

She'd never understood the definition of swooning before, but the prince made her feel weak-kneed and all-too-feminine. She didn't like it. Or him. She stepped back again.

"Shower?" he asked.

An image of the white robe slipping off his muscular shoulders and the opening widening at his chest, then lower, made her swallow. Hard.

If she didn't stop the fantasy in her mind, she was going to want to get in the shower with him.

No. NO. NO!

Her answer had to be no.

Getting Luc to the bathroom, let alone the shower,

meant being close to him. Touching him. That might sound the wake-up call to her hibernating ovaries. She didn't want her biological clock to start ticking for another ten years or so.

N-O.

"I—" Emily's voice cracked. She couldn't remember the last time a man had made her feel like this. She bit her lip.

A serious expression formed on Luc's handsome face. He glanced at Addie. "If Emma—"

"Emily." Getting worked up over a man who didn't remember her name was the definition of pathetic. She thought about her mom sticking with her dad for so many wasted years. With a flick of the proverbial switch, Emily's attraction for Prince Luc disappeared. She would never be like her mom.

Emily squared her shoulders. "My name is Emily."

"My mistake." His attention remained on Addie. "If Emily isn't up to the task, perhaps you'll help me shower."

Addie pinned him with a stare before Emily could say a word. "Got a death wish? Because if my husband—"

"Oh, right. Nick." Luc flashed Emily a this-will-be-fun smile. "Looks like you're it."

Lucky her. A prince with a hangover and short-term memory issues. Who wouldn't want this gig?

No worries. Saying no might have been her first instinct, but she couldn't. Until the prince was back at the villa and his search for a wife underway again, he was her responsibility. Don expected results. She wouldn't disappoint her boss.

What was the big deal helping Luc to the shower? He'd caught her off guard. She would be better prepared now. She appreciated the male physique. Never mind that Luc was a stranger or a prince. A naked guy was just that—naked. Nothing left to see except his backside. No reason to stress out.

Resolve firmly tucked into place, she raised her chin. "I'll help you."

So what if Prince Luc was nothing but trouble wrapped in a sexy package of movie star gorgeous looks, to die for wavy brown hair that curled at the ends, triathlete muscles and wiggle-you-out-of-your-panties charm?

She had this.

Emily glanced at Addie. "Call room service. Order lunch. Sandwiches. Salads. Coffee."

"I prefer tea." Luc sounded like he was speaking to a servant. "Earl Grey."

"Tea and coffee," Emily said to Addie.

His gaze narrowed. "No need to order coffee."

Jerk. Guess royals didn't consider the needs of peons, only themselves.

"What?" He raised his glass of water.

"You drink tea, but Addie and I drink coffee." Emily waited for an apology or simply an acknowledgment. None came.

He sipped his water.

She wasn't surprised he hadn't said a word. Prince Charming existed only in fairy tales. And even then, he left a lot to be desired. Emily preferred men who were uncomplicated and convenient and didn't act superior.

"Order whatever else you want," she said to Addie. "Use the phone in the sitting room."

"I'll stay in here." A worried look crossed Addie's face. They'd been friends since grade school, roommates for a few months last year. She knew Emily's patience was draining. "You might need something."

Emily tilted her head toward the doorway. "I'll yell if I do."

Addie hesitated, then walked out of the bedroom.

Luc watched her go. "She seems sweet. Nick's a lucky man."

"The luckiest." Though Addie hadn't made out too badly herself. The two belonged together.

"Are you married?" Luc asked.

His question surprised Emily. One glance at her ring finger, and he'd know the question. "No."

"Divorced?"

The word prickled. Divorce was a four-letter word in her vocabulary, and the last thing she'd ever be. Not that she'd tell Prince Nosy that.

She raised her chin. "My relationship status is none of your business."

"If we'd just met and were never going to see each other

again, I'd agree." He took another sip of water. "But you're here to help me find a wife. Knowing your relationship background is relevant to your job."

She'd bet matchmakers didn't have more successful relationships than the couples they introduced. Love was a crapshoot no matter who you were. But Emily was too tired to argue. She didn't have much to tell about her love life, and she doubted he would remember what she said.

"No current boyfriend." The last man she'd dated had been a pilot she saw whenever he flew into town, which wasn't much. The perfect arrangement until he'd wanted to get more serious. Her job didn't leave time for that. "Never engaged nor married."

"And they chose *you* to help me." Luc didn't sound impressed.

She didn't care what he thought. "Last year, I casted a honeymoon reality TV show that broke rating records. I also fixed problems during the production. My boss trusts me to do the same here."

Luc set the empty glass on the nightstand.

She stared down her nose at him. "Anything else you'd like to know?"

His mouth slanted in a lopsided grin. "Do you hate all men or is it just me?"

Her blood boiled. She pressed her lips together to keep from cursing. He was being obnoxious on purpose, trying to get a reaction and piss her off.

Five days. One hundred and twenty hours. Seven thousand two hundred minutes. That was how long she had to stay on this continent with him. After she returned home, she would be one step closer to making partner. She could put up with anything and anyone, including Prince Luc, for that to happen.

"Neither." She imagined business cards with her new title. That lowered her blood pressure. "The only things I hate are dentist visits, paying taxes, and fava beans."

"Fava beans?"

"Never quite developed a taste for them. You?"

"Does my answer matter to you?"

"I asked the question."

His gaze narrowed, as if he were trying to analyze her. "You're different."

"I've been called worse."

"What about nice?"

She shook her head once. "I'm too preoccupied with work to be described as nice."

"Doesn't that bother you?"

Emily shrugged. "My job is my focus. But I'm not mean. At least not on purpose."

That gave her an idea. Maybe she should rethink her interactions with the prince. If she approached him with more honey than vinegar in her words and deeds, things might go smoother. Luc seemed to get along with Addie, who was the definition of sweet. Emily was all for making an assignment easier.

"Come on." She hadn't smiled in hours, but she forced her lips to curve upward even if the action felt unnatural. "Let's get you into the shower. Nick will want to leave right away."

Luc stared at her with an odd expression. Puzzled or confused, Emily couldn't tell. She waited for him to say or do something. He didn't. Maybe his hangover had worsened.

"Change your mind about a shower?" she asked, unsure what was going on.

"No." He stood. Stepped. Swayed.

Timber. The word perched on the tip of her tongue. She wrapped her arm around his waist. "Hold onto me."

He leaned into her.

"I've got you." She grunted. Supporting his weight and keeping him steady wasn't easy, but she managed to keep him upright. "You're not going to fall."

Seconds, maybe a minute passed. She held onto him tight.

"Lost my balance." He steadied himself. "I'm okay now."

She didn't want to take any chances and kept hold of him. "Go slow, just in case. I don't want you to fall."

He gazed down at her. "I appreciate your concern."

Her heart thudded. That needed to stop. She couldn't let his words make her feel mushy and want to hear more.

Forget honey. Pour on the vinegar. "Well, if you fall and crack your head open, blood will go everywhere. I don't want my new shoes ruined. And we don't have time for a hospital visit."

"Good to have your priorities in order." He sounded more amused than upset. "Once again, your honesty is…refreshing."

"Jet lag must be shutting down my filter." She wondered, however, if his compliment was a subtle slam. Probably.

Five days.

Emily led him toward the bathroom ten feet away. The robe did little to hide his muscles underneath her palms. The guy was fit. He smelled pretty good after a night of drinking and needing a shower, too. "Small steps, please."

"I'm okay." Luc straightened, not fully, but her head still only came to his nose. He was taller than she realized. He let go of her. "Things are no longer spinning."

"Good." Emily loosened her grip, but kept her hands on him. Better safe than sorry. And touching him didn't suck. "You'll feel better after a shower."

He walked slowly, as if each step took concentration. "I appreciate your help."

"Who usually helps you the morning after partying?"

"No one," he said to her surprise. "I've been a prisoner at the villa for the past month. My taste of freedom may have gone to my head last night. Today is not a typical morning after."

Yeah, right. And she was a pretty princess waiting for her one true love to rescue her.

She eyed him warily. "So you normally just wake up and start partying again."

Luc laughed. The deep from the gut sound wrapped around her like a duvet. Cozy and warm.

Uh-oh. A royal snob and a prince of a jerk shouldn't make her feel this way, especially one who'd likely forgotten her name again.

"That's what the press would like you to believe, but it's far from the truth," he said. "I spend the day in bed sleeping it off."

"Alone?" Oh, no. She hadn't meant to say the word aloud. "Don't answer. It's none of my business."

"No, but I will answer anyway. If you hadn't arrived, I'd be asleep. Alone." Luc studied her as if she were a lifeform he'd never seen. "I'm no angel. I've never claimed to be, but I'm not a party animal intent on destroying my liver and spending my days in and out of rehab."

"You've been in rehab."

"I have not."

"I saw photos. Your parents confirmed you were there."

Pain flashed in his eyes. From his hangover or from the truth, she didn't now. But a part of her wished she could take back the words.

"You're in advertising. You should know better than to believe everything you see in the media."

Emily waited for him to say more and defend himself. He didn't. "That's all you're going to say."

"You've made up your mind."

She had. "But most people would—"

"I'm not most people." He stopped at the bathroom doorway. His hard gaze locked on hers. "I am a prince of Alvernia."

The pride in his voice and change in his posture sent a chill running through her. Regal was the only way to describe him.

"I will not discuss this further," he added.

His dismissive tone made her feel as if she'd been caught spreading rumors. Being nice had backfired. So had being her typical self. What now? Emily turned on the light in the bathroom.

A white marble countertop provided the perfect backdrop to the gold fixtures and large mirror. A toilet and a bidet were off to the left next to the tub.

He entered the bathroom. Squinted. "Is there a way to dim the light?"

"No. But I can turn off the light if you don't mind the dark."

"That will be best."

She lowered the toilet lid. "Sit until the water's warm enough."

He did.

She turned off the light, then propped open the door with a towel so the bathroom wouldn't be pitch black. She pushed back the shower curtain and turned on the tub

30

faucet. "Taking a bath in the dark will be safer than standing in the shower."

"I've never been one to take the safest path." He sounded like he might be smiling, but she focused on the warming water. "I'd rather shower."

Of course he would. She checked the water temperature. "Warm enough. Step into the tub. I'll close the curtain, then you can hand me your robe and switch the water stream from the faucet to the showerhead."

"Turn on the showerhead now. I'll disrobe, then get in."

She didn't want him in her face naked again. That would be too distracting, even with the lights off. "I prefer my plan."

"Yours is complicated. Mine is simple. You've seen me naked."

"Yes, but I'm trying to avoid impropriety. One wrong step, you hurt yourself. Imagine help arriving with you naked and me trying to explain what happened. Word would get out. The press would be nothing but hyperbole. That would mean trouble for both of us."

"Not to mention blood on your new shoes."

That made her smile. "Must avoid ruining the shoes."

A beat passed, then another. "Help me into the tub, hang up my robe, then step outside. Leave the door ajar. I'll call if I need assistance."

"You feel steady enough?"

He stood. This time he didn't sway. "Yes."

Thank goodness. She blew out a breath of air.

"That relieved?" he asked.

She helped him into the tub, then closed the shower curtain. "You have no idea."

"You do realize you're missing out on seeing me undress."

His playful tone made her laugh. Of course, he was right. His personality might leave a lot to be desired, but not his body. "I do. I'll just have to console myself."

"With champagne?"

She heard him taking off the robe. Tried not to think about him undressing. "Chocolate."

A bundle of fabric pushed around the edge of the curtain. She took the robe and hung it on the back of the door. "You're all set."

"I believe I am."

"I beg your pardon?"

"I have a feeling if anyone can find me a princess bride, it'll be you, Emily Rodgers."

A sense of pride swelled at his words. He'd remembered her name, too. "That's why they sent me. I won't let you down."

TWENTY MINUTES LATER, Luc found a white button-down shirt, gray pants, boxer briefs, a pair of gray socks, and a yellow tie on the bed. He dressed.

Emily must have done this. She seemed the type to have researched what outfit a royal should wear based on the time of day and destination.

Luc opened the door to the sitting area. His bodyguard, over six feet tall of inked muscles, leaned against the wall. The casual pose contradicted the man's warrior strength and quick reflexes.

Nick straightened. "Your tea's been steeping, sir."

"I thought we were beyond using *sir.*"

"Me, too. But then you ran away, bro."

And so it begins. "Saying I ran away makes me sound like I'm twelve."

"More like ten or eleven." Nick didn't crack a smile, nor did he sound amused. "I hope she was worth it."

Luc pictured sweet Vivianca with warm brown eyes, an infectious grin and dark blonde curly hair. "Most definitely."

"Is she royalty?"

"No." But that didn't stop her from calling herself a princess and wearing the tiara he'd given her for her birthday.

"She makes you happy."

Smiling, Luc sat near the tea service. "Very much so."

As did the other children helped by his Dream Big Alvernia foundation. In their young eyes, he was every bit a prince as his oldest brother, the Crown Prince, as royal as his Majesty, the king himself. Yesterday Vivianca had told Luc that she loved him. No one had said that to him in years. He doubted anyone else would say those words to him and mean them with the unconditional love of that beautiful child.

Nick unzipped a duffle bag. "Don't pull that crap again."

If Luc were needed, he wouldn't hesitate to do whatever he had to do to get there. "I can't make any promises."

"Figured as much." Nick pulled something silver from his back pocket. "That's why I brought handcuffs."

Luc picked up his cup of tea. "You'd have more fun if you used them on your beautiful wife."

Nick's nostrils flared. "Don't talk about Addie or—"

"I'll be known as Princess Lucy from here on out." Luc took a sip. "Emily warned me."

"Not surprised. She's the most organized person I know. Nothing gets by her."

Emily had appeared organized and competent, but she'd also spoken without thinking. The way her lips parted slightly had given her away, but her slip-ups made her seem human not a one-dimensional workaholic married to her job. "She's wound tight."

"She's been like that since she was a kid."

Luc couldn't imagine the woman as a little girl. She would have sent her dolls to get business and law degrees before going out on a first date. "She doesn't like me."

"Emily doesn't like many people, but she gets the job done."

No doubt. She had with him. Luc had more questions, but he didn't want Nick to take his interest in Emily the wrong way. "She's not the only one. Your wife gave me the death stare to make sure I received Emily's message."

"That's my girl." Nick's grin made him look almost nice.

Luc surveyed the sitting room over the lip of his cup. Empty plates. Half-filled coffee cups. No pretty faces to look at nor curves to admire. "Where are the ladies?"

"At the van. Along with the luggage, including yours. Traveling light these days?"

He ignored him, focused on the tea.

"Hungry?" Nick asked.

Luc's stomach clenched. The shower had helped, but he wasn't a hundred percent over the hangover. "Tea is enough."

"That's what you get after a two-day drinking binge."

"Not two days." Though he hadn't slept much after he arrived, but that wasn't due to partying. "Only last night."

"No need to lie. I'm your bodyguard, not your father."

Nick's tone reminded Luc of Emily's. No one believed him. "My father wouldn't be standing here calmly."

"He knows you're in Alvernia."

Luc bit back a curse. He sipped his tea without letting his emotions betray him. "What was His Majesty's reaction?"

Nick's hard gaze narrowed. "He was livid you'd put yourself in danger by not bringing security."

Livid, not worried or concerned. Typical. His siblings ignored his calls and texts. His parents had forbidden him to return to the palace without a royal fiancée. His biggest asset to his family was being the scapegoat. He took the blame and diverted attention for his oldest brother—the so-called happily married and upstanding Crown Prince Bernard— from drug rehab stints to one-night stands.

One big happy royal family.

Luc finished his tea. "No one is planning to hurt me. My oldest brother might be a target since he's heir to the throne, but I'm the youngest. Expendable."

"You're a prince from a powerful and wealthy family. You could have been kidnapped or set up by scam artists or a woman."

"I'm not a child ignorant of the ways of the world."

"No, but you're a man who likes to have too much fun."

"There's nothing dangerous about the fun I have."

"Don't test your luck." Nick's jaw jutted forward. "Next time you decide to take off, I won't be puking my guts out and you won't get as far. Handcuffs are not comfortable."

"You have experience wearing them?"

Nick's frown deepened. "This is nothing but a game to you."

Not really. A game had a winner, something that was out of reach for Luc. But others counted on him. With Emily Rodgers' assistance, he wouldn't let them down.

"What else would you call being paraded in front of royal women like a stallion in need of a brood mare?" Luc asked.

"Insane."

"Exactly."

But he would allow himself to be filmed by a reality TV crew in the name of D-U-T-Y. He had no other choice.

His father's ultimatum lay heavy on Luc's heart. The consequences of failing were too great. He would find a royal to marry. He set his empty cup on the table. "Let's go."

Nick handed him the duffle bag. "Wear these over your clothes and put whatever didn't get packed into the bag. We'll use the service elevator. A white van's parked outside the hotel's kitchen entrance. Emily will have the engine running."

"I pity anyone who crosses her path. Though watching her go after the paparazzi would be entertaining."

"There would be blood."

"Not while she's wearing new shoes."

Luc smiled, thinking about the ad exec turned royal matchmaker. He could see the gears turning in her brain as she tried to figure something out. He hoped she would be as analytical finding him a bride.

He had two weeks. Two weeks until filming ended. Two weeks until he needed to be engaged. Two weeks until life as he knew it would end if he failed.

Emily Rodgers had better not disappoint him.

Chapter Three

EMILY SAT IN the middle bench seat of the idling white van. The side door was open. A breeze carried the scents of basil and garlic from the hotel's kitchen. She wanted to nap, but checked her cellphone instead. Nearly twenty minutes had passed since she left Luc's hotel room. Nick had said he'd be down in ten. "Any word?"

"No text." Addie placed her cellphone in her pocket. "I hope they didn't run into trouble."

"I haven't seen anyone except the kitchen staff carrying out garbage." Emily glanced out the back of the van, saw no one, and faced forward. "My guess is the prince isn't cooperating."

"He's…"

"A pain in the butt."

"I was going to say handsome."

"Still a pain."

Addie shook her head, the way she'd done for as long as

Emily remembered. "Since when did you start calling handsome, naked guys pains? You wanted pictures of that surfer taking off his wetsuit in front of us last year."

"I would have taken them except you grabbed my phone. You better be careful talking about another man like that. What if Nick finds out?"

"I'm married, not blind. And that's what I'd have to be not to notice a bare-chested, hottie prince."

"I'll concede the point."

"You better since you were checking him out."

"Inspecting him." Emily spoke carefully, considering each word. She didn't want her friend to know how affected she'd been around Luc. Otherwise, Addie might decide to find Emily a date when they got home. No, thank you. "Looking for flaws that are keeping him from finding a wife."

"I wouldn't change anything about the guy, other than his drinking." Addie's nose crinkled. "But that might explain why he can't find a princess to marry."

Except the production crew hadn't mentioned any drinking issues during filming. "Maybe it's just him."

"You think?"

Emily nodded. "Consider the facts. Prince Luc is gorgeous, but a man needs more than a pretty face and incredible body. Women want their husbands to have the whole package. That means looking beyond the surface. Let's face it. His personality needs a complete overhaul. The guy's not only arrogant and obnoxious, but he's also—"

"Right here," a familiar royal voice said.

Heat rushed up Emily's neck. Every nerve ending stiffened. She glanced out the open door. Did a doubletake.

Luc wore a pair of stained, baggy, blue coveralls and plastic-rimmed glasses. A nametag on his pocket read Otto. He held the straps to a canvas duffle bag. Her pulse kicked up a notch. He looked completely different. Not so rock-her-world sexy, but real…approachable.

The thick glasses hiding the prince's gorgeous eyes and lashes weren't vintage hip. Her grandpa had worn those kind of frames when he read her funnies in the Sunday paper. Maybe that memory was why she found them so appealing on Luc.

Damp curls stuck out the bottom of a funny-looking cap, as if he suffered from both a bad hair day and a horrible cut. Funny, given his carefree style suited his features and looked good after waking from a dead sleep.

She could almost believe Luc was a manual laborer except for two things. His hands. No callouses and scars and clean fingernails. And his shoes. He wore dirty shoe coverings, but those didn't completely hide leather dress shoes that cost what a maintenance man earned in a week.

Still she gave Nick credit for coming up with the disguise on short notice while recovering from food poisoning. No wonder he was paid the big bucks.

"You're staring." Luc smiled widely. "Like what you see?"

"I like that you're dressed."

"Are you certain about that?" He reached for the zipper on his coveralls. "Most women prefer me undressed."

Addie laughed. So did Luc.

Emily ignored both of them. "Get in the van before anyone notices you."

"My mother wouldn't recognize me in this outfit."

"That's the point of a disguise. Though you might find some women prefer maintenance man Otto to Prince Luc."

"Name one."

His tone challenged Emily, but she'd die before naming herself. "Just sayin'."

He climbed inside. He leaned across her seat. His fresh scent circled her head. Not only soap. Something more. Him. Too bad she couldn't bottle the fragrance and start her own company. She would be set for life.

"Excuse me, ladies, for interrupting your conversation," he said.

His nearness sent Emily scooting back across the seat until she crashed into the side of the van.

A wicked smile spread across his face. "Or perhaps I'm not sorry since I'm arrogant and obnoxious."

His tone teased. Emily's shoulders hunched. The man pushed her buttons without having to try hard. Feeling out of control bothered her, reminded her of her childhood.

"Do you intend to give me a personality makeover before or after you introduce me to my future wife?" he asked.

If he had any manners or sense of decorum, he wouldn't have brought up what he'd heard. But, of course, he didn't and he had. "I'm—"

"Don't apologize." He moved to the last row and sat behind her, but the distance didn't keep his intoxicating scent from tickling her nose. "You calling me gorgeous makes up for the rest."

If Emily's cheeks were pink before, they burned now. Scorching hot. The more time she spent with him, the less she liked him. At this rate he would join her list of dislikes. Right between taxes and fava beans.

Addie laughed. "A speechless, blushing Emily. Well done, Luc. I should have been recording this."

Traitor.

Emily flexed her fingers to keep from balling her hands into fists. No way could she get herself out of this mess. Time to change the subject. "Where's Nick?"

As if on cue, the driver door opened. Nick jumped in the van. He buckled his seatbelt. "Right here."

Emily had known him for over two decades. The two good-looking guys in the van couldn't be more different. One she would trust with her life. The other she wouldn't trust with a goldfish. Well, if she had time for a pet.

Nick drove down the ramp to the street, then turned left. "Stay low until we're out of town, Luc."

The prince ducked so the seats hid him.

Emily glanced behind her seat at Luc. Based on how

comfortable he looked, she doubted this was the first time he'd hidden in a car or wore a disguise. "Next stop the airport."

He looked up at her. "We need to make a slight detour first."

"No."

"It won't take long."

"The jet is waiting for us." So was the production crew at the villa in Lake Como. A princess Emily had contacted in between flights would be arriving at the villa tomorrow. "We have to get to Italy."

"Non-negotiable." Luc's voice, firm and unyielding, carried through the van. "We stop, or I will not get on the plane."

"What's so important about stopping?" she asked.

"I have an obligation."

"To do what? Purchase champagne for the trip?"

His features hardened. "I promised someone I would say goodbye before I left."

"Vivianca?" Nick asked.

"Yes. She's expecting me."

Emily's fingernails dug into her palms. She should have known a female was involved. "You've taken too many chances as it is. What if someone sees you with her?"

"No one will. I give my word. The way I gave my word to Vivianca about saying goodbye."

His word wasn't worth much to Emily. The only four

she wanted to hear him say were "Will you marry me" to whatever princess would say yes. "What do you think, Nick?"

"Your call." Nick turned onto what looked like a highway. "But we need his cooperation here and in Italy."

She weighed the pros and the cons, but Nick made a good point. They didn't have much time to finish filming.

"Five minutes. That's all the time we have." She used her don't-mess-with-me voice. "You need to tell Vivianca you won't be returning to Alvernia for two weeks no matter what."

"But—"

"Non-negotiable." She wasn't taking any more grief from him. "If you'd rather go straight to the airport—"

"I'll tell her. Thank you, Emily."

Her name rolled off Luc's tongue with the slightest of accents and a musical sound. Her tummy tingled. Warmth spread through her veins.

Argh. She needed to go on more dates if a handsome guy saying her name while wanting to see another woman made her feel all girly inside. She would sign up for the next speed-dating event when she was back in San Diego. A little male company and she'd be good for another couple of months on her own.

"Tell Nick how to get there," she said.

Luc provided directions.

As they left the town, the road narrowed, and the traffic

decreased. Towering trees lined the side of the highway. The long branches had grown together to form a canopy across the road. Tall grass at the base of the trunks swayed in the breeze.

Pretty, but surreal. This could be a page out of a fairy tale picture book with the intense colors and greenery surrounding them.

"You can stop hiding," Nick said.

Luc sat. The silly cap remained on his head. "Have any of you been to Alvernia before?"

"No," Addie said. "None of us have."

That didn't stop Emily. "Based on my research, your country seems similar to Andorra, San Marino, Monaco, and Liechtenstein."

"Yes, but there are more differences than similarities. Alvernia has one of the top baking and pastry programs in the world. The Alps are a big draw, and tourism is our second largest industry after pastries."

He launched into a history lesson about how his country had picked the right side in some wars, the wrong side in others, and now remained neutral in international affairs, even though they maintained an army.

"The monarchy's sense of humor has fallen to an all time low, but so have unemployment levels," he continued. "Salaries keep increasing so no real complaints from the populace. A vocal few call for an end of aristocracy, but those cries die each time the quarterly financial numbers are released."

His knowledge and passion for his country surprised Emily. He tossed facts and figures around like an economics advisor. Amusing, given he was dressed as a blue-collar worker and his party reputation.

Had she misjudged the prince? Too soon to tell, but she recognized one thing. "You love Alvernia."

"Very much so." Affection sounded in his voice. "I would do anything for my country."

"That's obvious. Otherwise you wouldn't be on a reality TV show looking for a princess bride."

"A man must settle down eventually." His playful tone didn't quite match the hint of sadness in his eyes. "My Cinderella is out there. I just need to find her."

Maybe the guy wasn't that bad. "And when she's found, let's hope her fairy godmother puts in a good word for you."

His smile widened. "A wave of her magic wand might do the trick."

"Or Cupid's arrow." Having a princess fall in love with Luc would make things so much easier. "But in case those fail, I have a questionnaire that's supposed to help couples fall in love."

Luc shrugged. "Worth a try."

"You can't force love," Addie said.

"Maybe not." Emily wasn't sure if love was an extreme case of like and lust or something more. "But perhaps one can give love a shove in the right direction."

"Love doesn't have to enter into a marriage," Luc said matter of fact. "Having a relationship that's more like a business transaction is not unheard of in royal marriages."

"Don't lose hope." Turning, Addie smiled at the prince. "You never know what might happen."

They passed a gated entrance with a coat of arms on the wrought iron and colorful flags waving overhead.

"Is this the palace?" Emily asked.

"No, a private estate," Luc said. "Turn right at the gate and follow the dirt road until you come to a small cottage. Park in front. No need to pull over to the side. No one comes down this road."

"At least you hope not," Nick mumbled.

"They don't." Luc leaned toward the window, his nose close to the glass, like a child seeing snow fall for the first time.

She turned toward him. "You're excited to see Vivianca."

"Yes." His gaze didn't stray from the window. "I don't see her nearly enough."

Emily wondered if Vivianca knew how much the prince wanted to see her. No guy, not even Emily's father, had felt that way about her. Must be nice. Someday. Though finding a boyfriend was at the bottom of her To Do list. "I'm sorry you can't stay longer."

The words slipped out before she could stop them. Funny thing was she meant them. Weird. Very unlike her.

"I'll make the most of the five minutes I have," he said.

Nick drove slower. "Isolated out here."

"Yes, but only a short drive to town." Luc's breath fogged the window. "The location affords both privacy and convenience."

Questions circled through Emily's head. Had he put Vivianca in a house where they could meet unseen? If that were the case, why was he staying at the hotel alone instead of here?

A small house appeared. Wooden flower boxes filled with brightly colored blossoms hung in front of the brightly painted house's paned glass windows. A stone path cut a carpet of green grass in half. The animal-shaped topiaries and a Snow White-worthy life-sized wishing well reminded Emily of Disneyland, a place she hadn't been to since high school.

"What a cute cottage. Fairies should live here," Addie said.

"They do." Luc laughed. "Or so I've been told. I've yet to see one myself, but I keep hoping."

Fairies? Emily hoped he was just playing along, and not delusional. He had enough strikes against him.

"Are you going to change clothes?" she asked.

"No." He adjusted his nametag. "I'll need the disguise at the airport.

Nick parked. "Five minutes. Emily will go with you."

The thought of watching Luc make out with his girlfriend unsettled Emily. "You go, Nick. I'll stay with Addie."

"No." Nick looked around, as if he expected a photographer to pop out of the wishing well like a Jack-in-the-box. "This could be a ruse for the prince to escape."

A muscle throbbed at Luc's jaw. "It's not."

"If someone shows up—" Nick continued as if Luc hadn't spoken "—I'll need you to hide the prince."

Luc exhaled loudly. "The prince can hear you and is capable of hiding himself from photographers, ninjas, and princess wannabes."

"Keep your cellphone in hand," Nick instructed Emily. "Be ready."

"The prince is getting out of the van." Luc did.

He sounded frustrated. No doubt, Emily's presence would ruin his plans for a quick romantic rendezvous. She hopped out of the van and caught up to him.

The scent of wildflowers hung on the air. Sweet, but not overpowering. Hummingbirds zipped by one of the planters. A silver unicorn wind chime cling-clinked-clanged in an appealing rhythm. Bright green moss grew between the path's stones.

Almost everything she'd seen in Alvernia seemed to be straight out of storybook or fairy tale film adaption. She half-expected to see seven dwarfs stroll by or be greeted by a talking rabbit. Maybe a magic mirror inside would show her Luc's future wife. Emily crossed her fingers.

For being jet lagged, she felt unexpectedly playful. "This is the perfect fairy house, but I could imagine a few hobbits hanging around this place, too."

"As long as the goblins and Smaug the Dragon stay away. Only goodness and light are allowed here, never any dark." Luc knocked on a bright purple painted door.

"Who's there?" a hesitant feminine voice asked.

"Luc."

The door swung open. A twenty-something woman with dark circles under her eyes stood in the doorway.

"Oh, sir. I didn't recognize the van." The words rushed out in English. Her accent sounded Australian. She wore black yoga pants, a flour stained T-shirt, and mismatched socks. She looked more like a worn-out mom than the paramour of a prince. "I hadn't heard from you and was worried."

"I apologize for not calling." He touched the woman's shoulder. "When was the last time you slept?"

"It's been a long day, after a longer night." Weariness filled the woman's voice. "Tonight will be better. I hope."

Lines creased Luc's forehead. "How is she?"

"Been asking for you since she woke."

He walked into the house without an invitation.

Emily smiled at the woman. "Hello. I'm Emily Rodgers."

"I'm Gretchen Barton. Please come inside." She opened the door wider. "Any friend of Prince Luc's is welcome, but excuse the mess."

Emily didn't consider herself his friend, but the less she said the better. She hadn't a clue what was going on. She stepped inside, curious for answers.

Hand-drawn pictures made by children hung on the wall. One of fairies flying around a wishing well caught her eye. Lots of pinks and purples and sparkles covered the paper.

Toys lay scattered on the floor. Stuffing stuck out of the back of a well-loved pink bear. One of the eyes was missing. Just like Emily's Miss Mousie cat.

The scent of freshly baked treats filled the house. Emily's mouth watered and her stomach grumbled.

"You have a lovely home." A crayon drawing of a girl holding a man's hand captured Emily's attention. A pink heart surrounded the pair. The word *daddy* was scribbled on the bottom. "I love the artwork."

"My daughter Vivianca, is quite the artist."

Daughter, huh? Emily had more questions than answers. "How old is she?"

"Seven."

That explained the drawings and toys. "Are you related to the prince?"

"No, but he treats us like family. My daughter calls him our fairy godfather. His foundation helped us after my husband was killed and Vivianca injured by a hit-and-run driver. I'm from Australia and have no family locally. Prince Luc moved us into this house and has become a dear friend." Gretchen's respect and affection for the prince was clear in her voice. "I don't know how I'll repay his generosity."

"I had no idea the prince was personally involved with his charity's recipients."

Gretchen nodded. "Very hands-on with all of us."

Excitement shot through Emily. The prince's foundation work would be a huge boon for the show. Princesses might be more willing to meet with Luc if they saw a caring side to him.

Gretchen continued toward the back of the house. "The prince checks in with Vivianca every day no matter where he is and he comes when she asks him to visit."

A missing puzzle piece clicked into place. "Did your daughter ask Prince Luc to visit this week?"

"Yes. She was hospitalized with an infection. He couldn't come immediately, but once he arrived, he stayed by her side until she was discharged yesterday. The man is a saint. So kind and patient with the children."

Not child. Children, as in plural. Emily wiggled her toes. "Is he with your daughter now?"

Gretchen nodded. "In the dining room, though we've never eaten there."

A minute later, Emily understood why. A hospital bed took up the space. A young girl with dark blonde curls and brown eyes lay on a pink sheet under a fuzzy pink blanket. Half a dozen stuffed animals surrounded her. A TV hung on the wall next to a video game system. A wheelchair was nearby.

Luc was sitting on the bed. His attention was focused on

the girl, who smiled up at him like he was the center of her universe.

Vivianca touched his nametag. "Your name isn't Otto."

"This is my disguise so I could come see you." He tilted his cap to one side. "What do you think?"

She giggled. "You don't look like a prince."

"That, my princess, is the point of the disguise. Though the cap is ridiculous, don't you think?"

She laughed. "Very silly."

Luc raised the girl's hand and kissed the top of it. "I will do what it takes to see you."

Vivianca sighed.

Emily's heart melted. Luc's tender bedside manner contradicted what she knew—well, assumed—about him. Hard to believe an hour ago he was lying naked in bed with a hangover.

"Someone wants to meet you," Gretchen said to her daughter.

Luc glanced over. "I brought a visitor with me today, Vivianca. I'd like to introduce you to Emily Rodgers."

Emily approached the bed. "Nice to meet you, Vivianca."

The girl stared up with wide eyes. Her pink lips formed a perfect o. "You must be a princess dressed in disguise."

"No, I'm just plain Emily."

Vivianca's brow furrowed. "Prince Luc says all girls are princesses."

Oops. Emily wasn't familiar with children. She'd been an only child and never babysat. Well, except for her mother.

"I'm from America," Emily said. "We don't have royalty, but I've been told there are princesses everywhere else. Like here in this room. Am I right?"

Dark blonde curls bounced from the enthusiastic nodding.

"I have a tiara and a scepter. A dress and a hooded cap." Excitement filled Vivianca's young voice. "Oh, and sparkly pink shoes, but I can't wear those until my legs aren't broken anymore. I am a fairy princess, but I haven't visited my fairies because they live outside and I'm stuck inside. But I see them flying by the window."

"When the weather warms, you shall be outside with your fairies, princess," Luc said without missing a beat. "Your subjects will cheer your return with fanfare and flowers."

Vivianca's narrow shoulders shimmied. "I love flowers. And I love you, Prince Luc."

"I love you." He kissed the girl's forehead. "I wish I could stay longer, but Emily and I must get to the airport."

The girl thrust forward her lower lip in an enormous, adorable pout. "When will you be back?"

"Two weeks, but keep your tablet handy so we can chat."

"You must have important work to do."

A beat passed. And another. "Very important. As do you. I cannot wait to see your progress when I return."

"One day I will dance again."

The gentle way he touched Vivianca's face brought tears to Emily's eyes.

"You shall dance again, princess," he said. "We will dance together."

Emily's heart pounded in her ears. She had no idea what she was witnessing, but she didn't want the moment to end.

Forget Italy. Bring the camera crews here. Any princess—make that any woman—who saw the prince with Vivianca would propose to him on the spot. Emily might have fallen for him a little herself. Her insides felt warm and gooey.

"So glad I had this chance to visit," Emily said.

"Goodbye." Vivianca's lowered lip trembled. "I will miss you, sir."

"And I you." He pointed to his heart. "But you are here with me always. And I'm with you, even if we can't be together."

"Like Daddy."

"Yes, like your daddy."

A weight pressed against Emily's chest. She couldn't breathe. If only her father had said those words to her. He wasn't dead, but he might as well be. He'd chosen to have another family, one where she wasn't welcome.

"Thank you for coming." Gretchen hugged the prince, then she handed him a paper bag. "We baked sweets for your trip."

That explained the delicious smell in the house.

"I helped," Vivianca said.

He handled the bag as if it held rare jewels, not home-made baked goods. "If you need anything…"

Gretchen nodded. "Nice to meet you, Emily."

"You, too." She forced the word out her tight throat. A jumble of thoughts rattled her jet-lagged brain. Who was Prince Luc really? Why did this child mean so much to him? What would be the best way to use this on the show?

He touched the girl's cheek once more. "Sweet dreams, my princess. Until we see each other again."

"That'll be on-line tonight or tomorrow."

Luc laughed. "You're much too smart for me."

Vivianca beamed brighter than the neon lights on the Las Vegas strip.

"We'll see ourselves out." Luc placed his hand at the small of Emily's back.

She stiffened, unused to anything more than a touch on the arm or shoulder from anyone, but she quickly relaxed. The gesture wasn't possessive, but seemed natural.

Emily stepped outside. The wind chime provided a song, and the floral scent seemed stronger. More birds chirped.

Luc followed her, closing the door behind him.

She glanced over her shoulder. "Is Vivianca part of your—"

"I know you have questions, but please, do not ask any in front of Nick and Addie. We'll talk later. In private."

"That's fine. I won't say a word." For now.

Walking to the van, she pictured Luc as a husband and father. Something an hour ago, she would have never considered. If she felt that way, so would other women. The princesses and royalty on the list needed to see this side of the prince.

A bluebird landed on the wishing well, as if this were an animated princess film, not real life.

A sign?

She was the last person to get carried away with fanciful thoughts, but after witnessing the prince's kindness and compassion the urge to make a wish was strong.

If one true love does exist, my wish is for Prince Luc to find his before filming ends.

There. She'd made the wish. Not that anything would come from it. But an unexpected thought pounded through her brain.

Too bad the glass slipper couldn't fit her foot. The shoe would not only be a wonderful addition to her collection, but she had a feeling if anyone could make her believe in Prince Charming and happily ever afters, it just might be Luc.

Chapter Four

L UC NAPPED ON the drive to the airport. He slept during the flight. Now in the back of a limousine on the way to the villa, he stayed awake, watching his two female travel companions.

"I can't believe we're in Lake Como." Addie stared out the window at the passing scenery with a genuine look of awe.

Her appreciation of new sights and sounds—from the captain chairs on the jet to the classical music playing in the car—reminded Luc of a fresh-faced teenager, not a married woman.

"There is much to see." Though Luc noticed Emily had her tablet out again. She only wanted to work. He wondered when she relaxed. So far today, she hadn't.

"If you like cathedrals, you'll want to visit *Duomo di Como*." He tried to imagine where tourists might want to go. "You don't want to miss the number one attraction, the *Villa*

Balbianello. A stunning location. A scene for a Star Wars movie was filmed there."

Addie leaned forward. "The wedding scene, right?"

Luc nodded. He found her enthusiasm contagious. Perhaps Emily would enjoy a tour. "Let's go sightseeing tomorrow. Take a boat ride. Ride the *Pigra* Cable Car. Stroll gardens. Explore museums."

Emily didn't look up from her tablet. That irritated him. A woman should find him more interesting than the words on a screen, even if her work would benefit him.

"Please, I'd love that. I want to see everything." Addie tapped her feet. "George Clooney has a place here, right?"

"Yes, but stay away from celebrities. Paparazzi will be following them." Nick's voice held a warning. "If you and Emily want to sightsee, that's fine, but you'll have to go on your own. Luc needs to stay out of sight."

Luc's muscles tightened. He wasn't used to being under house arrest. He couldn't give up his freedom without a fight.

"A-list movie stars are at the top of the paparazzi's lists and who they follow." He used his most convincing tone, the one that had talked his parents into sending him to school in England. "Royalty from small countries like mine is near the bottom in a star-studded locale like Lake Como."

"Not taking any chances." Nick's firm tone said this wasn't up for debate or a vote. "Two more weeks, then you're free."

Luc wasn't amused. "I hope to be engaged by then."

"You will be." Emily's tablet lay on her lap. "But *free* could be a relative term, depending on your bride-to-be."

He hadn't expected her to make a joke, and he liked seeing she had a sense of humor.

"Ball and chain, baby," Nick joined in.

Addie elbowed him. "Ha-ha. Not."

Emily looked at Nick, then made a face. "I doubt any princess would want to be described like that."

Luc grinned at the way the women teamed up. The best part? He wasn't the one in trouble. But he couldn't let his jailer face the duo alone.

"No, but the words fit a few," he agreed. "Such as my oldest sister, Bettina."

Emily's smile brightened her face. Pretty, dare he say borderline beautiful without her serious eyebrows drawn together and her lips pinched in a you're-kidding-me look.

Beauty and brains was a combination he ignored. Interesting, yes, but intelligent women were more complicated. Complicated meant less fun. He liked having a good time.

Laughter filled Emily's gaze. "You realize we'll be meeting Princess Bettina at the engagement presentation. We'll be able to see if you're right or not."

Not only complicated, but trouble. In the time since Emily Rodgers had woken him, Luc learned four things about her.

She was sharp—book smart and common sense wise.

Her comeback to Vivianca about no princesses living in America had been brilliant and kept an injured child's fantasy alive. He couldn't wait to see Emily's choice of bride candidates.

She was an unapologetic workaholic. Being jet lagged after transatlantic travel hadn't stopped her from pulling out her tablet and mini-keyboard the minute they boarded the jet. She never seemed to relax.

She was also curious. He didn't need a PhD in psychology to know the number of questions she had for him were growing exponentially. But she hadn't asked him anything since leaving the cottage. He appreciated her restraint and would tell her what he could without admitting that his family needed him to be seen as a royal screw-up, not a caring philanthropist, for the sake of the monarchy.

She was nicer than he thought and nicer than she claimed to be. She'd been friendly and shed tears, then tried to wipe her eyes without anyone noticing. But he had.

The fact he'd taken so much time cataloging a woman he'd just met was interesting in and of itself.

"Is there anything you'd like to see in Lake Como, Emily?" he asked.

Her gaze zeroed in on him. "Your engagement ring on the finger of a princess, countess, or duchess."

He could add one-track mind to his list of things about her. "I'd like to see that too. And don't forget the ring finger of a baroness, marchioness, viscountess, and viceroy also works."

Emily tucked her tablet in her large purse. "Wouldn't that be vicereine?"

He was impressed she knew the term. "Viceroy is gender-neutral so either can be used."

"Learn something new every day." She zipped her bag. "With so many feminine royals to choose from, we're bound to succeed. The project seemed to have overwhelmed the royalty consultant. She should have had dates lined up prior to filming, not been so haphazard in her approach. Many royals had been left off the original princess list. I created a database for us to use, and I've already contacted twenty women."

"When was the last time you failed?" Luc asked.

She rubbed her lips together. "I can't remember.

"That's what I thought."

The limo stopped. Luc climbed out of the car.

The villa was an imposing structure, rectangular with three stories of public rooms, dining areas, bedroom suites, and two kitchens. The luxurious accommodations were meant to impress potential brides rather than make his life more pleasant. But since he couldn't leave the premises, he would have to make the most of activities available here.

He stood in front of Venetian double doors. The scent of hanging wisteria—sweet like a freshly cut spring bouquet—mocked him. A glance over his shoulder at the lake heckled his lack of choices on what was the antithesis of a royal holiday.

The natural beauty couldn't hide the truth. This place was nothing but a prison, one with cameras pointed at him 24/7. His visitor times brought potential fiancées, women he was supposed to impress with his wit, humor, and good looks. Maybe they should put him into solitary confinement and throw away the key.

Duty. Honor. The foundation's children.

He stepped inside. The smell reminded him of home, a mix of antiques, tapestries, lemon oil, and floral arrangements.

Symmetrical staircases on either side leading off a center aisle greeted him. Luxurious red runners trimmed with gold lined the stairs.

Luc removed the coveralls, glasses and cap. He tucked in his shirt, adjusted his tie and brushed his fingers through his hair. He would save the disguise for future use. No one had looked at him twice.

Except Emily.

He nearly laughed. She must be a fan of laborers not royalty, but that kind of person would fit with her work habits.

"Oh my goodness." Addie sounded breathless. "Look at the paintings on the ceilings and the moldings." She looked up and spun slowly. "This is a real life Pemberley."

"Yes, only Italian in design, not English." Luc glanced at Nick. "Though you brought your own Mr. Darcy."

Nick laughed. Emily too.

Speaking of which, time to speak with her about Vivianca.

"Leave your bags for the staff to attend to," Luc said to Emily. "I want to show you one of the gardens."

Her mouth slanted. "Now?"

"Yes. Do you have other plans?"

Hesitation flashed in her tired eyes, but she set her purse on her suitcase. "No. Lead the way."

He took the left staircase, led her through one of four sitting areas, then outside. The sun reflected off the tile, and he loosened his tie. "You're going to get warm wearing black."

She shrugged. "The color travels well. I'll survive."

He studied her clothing. Remembered something from a trip to Paris last month. "Your shirt reminds me of something I saw during Fashion Week."

"It's from a new designer." Her gaze narrowed. "You're into women's clothing?"

"Women models."

"I see."

Did she? If so, that would be another strike against him. He headed toward the garden he'd discovered his first day at the villa. "Do you cook?"

"That's a non sequitur."

"I want to show you the kitchen garden."

"If microwaving frozen meals and reheating take-out count, then I cook. Otherwise, I don't."

"I don't. Unless you count making reservations, but someone does that for me." Though he knew how to make grilled cheese sandwiches. Andre, a boy his foundation helped, loved those, but Emily didn't need to know that.

Luc went down a short staircase carved out of rocks. Creeping thyme with small lavender flowers grew along the edge and cascaded down the steps. He used to follow the palace gardeners around when he was little. "But I like knowing where my food comes from."

He stepped onto a flat area with rows of vegetable plants and fruit trees. "The villa has ten gardens. This one is used to make our meals."

"A sustainable villa." She sounded impressed.

He'd been. "Take whatever you like. The figs are especially good. If you like figs."

"I do." Emily inhaled deeply.

Her shirt separated in the gap between the buttons giving him a glimpse of black lace. Sexy. Unexpected. Very sexy.

She exhaled. "I smell lavender."

"The flagstone path to the left leads to a herb garden." Maybe they should head down there where she could smell more plants. "There are clippers to cut your own."

She gave the trail a two-second glance, then looked at him. "So Vivianca…"

Right to the point. Luc walked between two rows of plants, and Emily followed. He needed to be cautious with what he said. Too much was at stake to tell her the whole truth.

"Vivianca is one of the children assisted by my foundation called Dream Big Alvernia. I met her last year after her accident."

"How many children do you help?" she asked.

The question was not unexpected. They shared a common goal, but their reasons for wanting to succeed were different. Their methods would be too. "You and I need to reach an understanding about my foundation."

She bent over and pushed the green top of a carrot out of the path. "What kind of understanding? I'm here to make sure the show is a success. The more I know about you and your foundation, the better I'm equipped to find you a bride."

What had she said earlier? A true professional. He wondered what was in this for her—a raise, maybe a promotion. Truth was, he didn't care. Protecting his family and the foundation were his priorities.

"I want the show to be a success." He watched her smile widen. "But Vivianca, the other children, and the foundation are off-limits from the show."

Emily's expression fell. "That's...stupid."

He hadn't expected that much honesty. "Not from where I stand."

"Then take a step to your right so you have a new perspective."

She sounded not only annoyed, but also upset. "My perspective is fine. Your motivation for wanting to use my foundation and the children concerns me."

"My priority on the show is no different from any project I work on—to have a successful outcome." She walked toward him, her shoulders back and her chin lifted. "In order to do that, I need to sell you—past, present, and future—to the princesses. What you're doing, how you're helping these children and their families, will impress a woman."

"Are you impressed?"

"Yes, and surprised as hell about that. That tells me my instinct is spot on. Your interactions with these children is the perfect way to let princesses see your potential as a husband and a father, not just a fun date for New Year's Eve."

Pride puffed his chest. The foundation was a topic he'd never discussed with anyone outside his staff. Hearing Emily's view made him stand taller and wish he could tell people. But his family needed his reputation to be tarnished for a little while longer. "Imagine how happy my future wife will be when she finds out about it."

"That's only if you find a woman to marry." Emily's voice rose like a television commercial that kept getting louder to grab your attention. "You can't buy the kind of positive PR and praise you'll receive if you go public."

She didn't understand. "I'm not doing this for accolades."

Her head tilted. "Why are you doing it?"

She thought so little of him. He didn't know why her opinion mattered.

"Helping Alvernians, especially her youngest citizens, is the right thing to do." His voice came out more forceful than he intended, but he wanted to get his point across. What he did was private. "No one needs to know about the foundation. Not the public nor the show nor my family—"

Damn, he hadn't meant to say that.

Two lines formed above the bridge of her nose. "Your family doesn't know?"

He stood in the shade of a lemon tree. "My parents and siblings believe the fundraising events are an excuse to throw a party. They wrongly assume the donations are funneled to other charities."

She came toward him. "Why haven't you told them?"

He fingered a leaf. The top was smooth, but ridges lined the bottom.

Emily touched his arm. "Why?"

"No one has asked."

A beat passed. And another. "I'm asking."

His gaze met hers. Focused. Locked.

Luc saw no pity in her eyes, only compassion and interest and something unexpected…respect. A connection he didn't understand drew them together.

She squeezed his arm. "Please tell me about Dream Big Alvernia."

The air was cooler in the shade, but his temperature shot

up, maybe twenty degrees. His awareness of this woman kept increasing. Her palm on him. The breaths she took.

Focus.

This is about the children, not me.

Or her.

"I have a staff." He cleared his dry throat. "They care what happens to these children, are willing to put in extras hours to help the families."

"What do they do?"

He half-laughed. "A better question would be what don't they do."

Smiling, Emily lowered her hand and picked a fig from a nearby plant. He missed her touch. "Going public with Dream Big Alvernia is the right move. You'll reinvigorate your bride search. Princesses will be proposing to you."

He laughed at her tunnel vision. "You are driven. I'm lucky to have you on my side."

"Then let me help you. Advertising is what I do. I'm damn good at it, too."

"You're modesty is remarkable."

"Modesty gets you fired in my business." She wiped the fig with the inside of her shirt. A band of ivory skin flashed. "A coordinated campaign will help your search for a wife and tap into a larger donor pool so your foundation will thrive."

"One of these days it may come to that, but not today." He would have no choice but to do as she suggested if he failed to find a wife, and his father disowned him. "Do not mention the foundation or children to anyone. Understand?"

Emily didn't say anything. Her teeth dragged back and forth across her lower lip.

"Promise me," he said.

A beat passed. And another. She looked up at him. "If mentioning the foundation is the only way to marry you off—"

"We'll discuss our options then."

Her lips pursed. She looked both haughty and kissable.

He smiled, thinking about how she would taste. Warm, more savory than sweet, perhaps with a touch of spice and a dash of vinegar. Her kiss would likely surprise him, like the woman herself.

Emily's mouth twitched like she wanted to say something.

He had a feeling Emily would be red-faced furious if she found out he was thinking about her kiss. "What?"

"You're making a big mistake."

"Perhaps." He appreciated her willingness to state her opinion, even if he didn't agree with her. "But this is my mistake to make. I will take the blame if I fail."

And somehow try to make sure no one else experienced the fallout.

IN HER SUITE that evening, Emily opened her bag and pulled out an old stuffed animal. The cat's worn fur looked more gray than white, but she adored Miss Mousie.

Emily held up the toy. Only one whisker remained. Both eyes had been replaced more times than she could remember. But Miss Mousie went everywhere with Emily and knew all her secrets.

"Look how the other half lives. We could get lost in this room. A good thing we're only staying five days or we might not ever want to go home."

Home was a one-bedroom apartment located a short distance from her office. Emily placed Miss Mousie on the bed and then changed into pajamas.

A knock sounded.

Who could that be? Maybe the villa's housekeeper wanted to put a candy on the pillow. Emily was never too tired for chocolate.

She opened the door, clutched the handle. "Luc."

He held a tray with a small plate of cookies and a steaming mug. The cookies didn't look like the traditional chocolate chip ones she used to make with her grandmother.

"Vivianca called me to see how you liked the cookies. I didn't realize I was supposed to share. So here I am, milady, with cookies and a glass of warm milk for you."

Who did this? Probably the same kind of guy who dropped everything to sit with an injured or sick kid all night because they'd asked. "Come in."

His gaze ran the length of Emily. He smiled. "Men's flannel pajamas."

"Huh?"

He walked to the table by the window. "I was hoping you'd be wearing a see-through nightie from Victoria's Secret."

Emily laughed. "If I were, I wouldn't have opened the door."

He raised a brow. "Sure about that?"

His voice teased, and she would have loved to say yes except she wasn't one hundred percent certain. That bothered her.

Luc placed the plate and cup on the table. "Your nightcap is served."

"I didn't think princes were so self-sufficient given you don't make your own dinner reservations."

"After years of watching butlers, you pick up a few things." He pulled out a chair for her. "Have a seat."

She sat. "Would you like to join me?"

Luc sat opposite her. "I was hoping you would ask."

"You only brought one cup of milk."

"Showing up with two glasses and in my pajamas might be presumptuous."

"You don't wear pajamas."

Wicked laughter lit his eyes. "Exactly."

Trouble, she reminded herself. Enjoy the sweets and forget about the man. Emily took a cookie covered in powdered sugar and crushed nuts.

She ate a bite. "Delicious."

"I told you Alvernia is known for their pastries."

"Gretchen is from Australia."

"She was attending a baking program when she got married. After she graduated, she worked at one of the top bakeries, but quit after the accident."

"What's wrong with Vivianca's legs?" Emily asked.

"Multiple fractures. Nerve damage. She requires more surgeries."

"She mentioned dancing again."

"She was on her way home from a ballet lesson when they were hit."

Emily wrapped her hands around the mug. Maybe the milk would heat her hands. "Will Vivianca dance again?"

"I hope so." Luc picked up a cookie that resembled a snickerdoodle. "The doctor's prognosis is vague, but Gretchen believes Vivianca's recovery will go better if she's working toward a goal. Even if that goal might have to change as we learn more about the condition of her legs."

"I wish there was something I could do."

"There is." Luc took out his cellphone. "Pick up another cookie so I can send a picture to Vivianca. I'm sure she's waiting for one."

Imagining what might make a seven-year-old smile, Emily struck a pose.

His grin widened. "So you're not always professional. You know how to have fun."

"There's a time and place for fun."

"Glad it's with me tonight."

Her, too. This was the closest thing she'd had to a date in over two months. She bit into the cookie, then sipped her milk.

What was she thinking? The word date didn't belong in any sentence about the prince. Time to get back to business.

"How many other children did you speak with tonight?" she asked.

"Are you asking out of curiosity or because you want information about the foundation?"

"Mainly curiosity," she admitted. "If you'd rather not tell me, that's fine. I won't keep asking, but I'd love to know more. What you're doing for the kids is wonderful."

"Thank you."

The gratitude in his eyes touched something deep inside her. Emily forced herself to look away. She yawned. "Excuse me."

"The travel is catching up with you."

"Caught up and passed me, I think."

A text sounded on his phone. He laughed. "Vivianca says your pajamas are cute, but you look tired and I should tuck you into bed."

Emily placed her cup on the table. "Maybe if I was seven."

"How old are you?"

"Twenty-eight."

"An older woman."

She wasn't surprised he was younger. "How old are you?"

"Twenty-five."

"I'm ancient compared to you."

"A good thing there's no age limit on tuck-ins." He stood. "I don't have to tuck you in, but you need to sleep. Come on, get in bed."

Having Luc walk her to a romantic queen-sized four-poster canopy bed with lace panels might have worried her if she wasn't so tired and having a hard time keeping her eyes opened.

He pulled back the sheets. "Climb in."

"I can do this myself. I'd rather do it."

"I know. But I'm here." He patted the mattress. "You don't have to."

Her heart bumped. She hesitated, torn between logic and desire. Then decided not to listen to her head for once and got into bed.

He held up Miss Mousie. "Who's this bad boy?"

Oh, no. Emily hoped she was too tired to blush. "That's, um, Miss Mousie."

"Excuse me. Miss M. You are not a bad boy." Luc looked at the stuffed animal. "But I see you're well loved."

He placed the cat on the pillow, then kissed Emily's forehead the way he'd kissed Vivianca's.

Emily imagined what his kiss might taste like. Probably better than the cookies. On that note…

"Thanks. For the cookies, milk, and tuck-in."

Luc pulled up the blankets and covered her. "Anytime."

She snuggled against the pillow. Comfy, cozy, content. "See you here at bedtime tomorrow night."

He laughed. "It's a date."

What had he said? Her eyelids fluttered. Darkness surrounded her. Had the lights been turned off?

"Sweet dreams, Cinderella."

The warm, male voice wrapped around her like a hug.

Was she asleep? Must be dreaming or she wouldn't be thinking about Luc. A fitting line from Romeo and Juliet came to mind. "Goodnight, goodnight! Parting is such sweet sorrow, That I shall say goodnight till it be morrow."

LUC STOOD NEXT to Emily's bedside, aware of her breathing and his. The in-control, organized ad exec had turned into Sleeping Beauty. No prick of a spinning wheel required—only hours of travel, frustration, and work.

He'd contributed to all three, especially the second. For that he was sorry. She was trying to do her job, and like it or not, he needed her help. At least she'd enjoyed the cookies and warm milk before her energy level drained like an overused cellphone.

He watched her.

The blanket rose and fell evenly. Blonde hair spread across the white pillowcase.

He wanted to touch a strand, but kept his hands against

his side. Staying here while she slept was weird enough. He'd done this with the children from the foundation, but never a woman.

She looked serene. The adjective surprised him, given how she'd acted earlier, but was fitting given her Mona Lisa smile and the artwork hanging on the walls. He wondered what she was dreaming about.

Him? Not likely. He almost laughed. Probably her job.

No, that wasn't fair.

Emily showed glimpses that she wasn't a diehard workaholic. Traveling with an old stuffed animal seemed out of character, but adorable. And her reciting a line from *Romeo and Juliet* hinted at a romantic heart.

Something tingled deep in his stomach.

He looked away. None of those things mattered. She was a stranger sent into his life to help him with a difficult situation. Nothing more.

Yet here he was in her room while she slept. Time to get out of here.

Luc turned off the lights, walked out of her room, and closed the door behind him. Best to stay out of here in the future. Distractions, especially this intriguing American, weren't allowed, even if they were…tempting. He had a duty to fulfill. Nothing could get in his way.

Or his father's threat would become a reality.

Chapter Five

T HE NEXT MORNING, Luc found himself alone in the villa. He saw staff, but no sign of the production crewmembers, Nick, Addie or…Emily.

The determined, get-the-job-done set of her chin contradicted the dreamy way she'd looked sleeping. He'd been thinking about her since last night. Not sexual thoughts, either. That confused him.

He didn't have many female friends. The women in his life fell into neat categories: relatives, potential lovers, former lovers, foundation staff or mothers of children the foundation helped. Few fell outside those labels, but he couldn't fit Emily into one of them. Maybe he would when he saw her again.

Luc glanced into the sitting room decorated in pale yellows and grays. No sign of anyone. He checked the drawing room. Empty, too.

Where was everyone? Emily?

He went into the music room. The French doors leading to the terrace were open. Laughter sounded outside.

Luc stood in the doorway. A breeze was blowing, but the temperature was pleasant. Perfect spring weather. If only he were on holiday and not in a search to save his place in his family and most importantly, the foundation.

Dylan—the sound guy—was working on cables strung across lounge chairs. Underneath a pool cabana, the three other members of the production crew—Brad, Conrad and Wes—were staring at monitors. Emily stood with them. She laughed.

Luc's pulse spurted though he didn't know why. Perhaps he was tired since he'd woken before noon. Or maybe he wanted to forget about finding a wife and have a fling instead. Letting the villa's romantic setting go to waste would be a crime. Not that Emily would be willing.

I'm trying to avoid impropriety.

Emily rubbed the back of her neck. The motion made her chest stick out.

Her fitted T-shirt showed off delicious curves hidden by her clothes and pajamas yesterday, but ones he'd experienced up-close-and-personal when he'd fallen on her. A taste would be the perfect first breakfast course, better than a bowl of cut fruit or yogurt topped with granola and fresh berries.

Perhaps he could convince her to have a little fun.

With him.

Emily might not be his type, but he'd happily place her

in the potential lover category. Her above-the-knee skirt emphasized her long, toned legs. She didn't seem the type to hang out in a gym, but he imagined she power walked the hallways of her office.

Luc stepped onto the terrace. No one seemed to notice him. Not surprising. As a child, he would have thought himself invisible, if not for his mother and the palace staff.

Emily pointed at the monitor. "You captured the vibe of the villages around the lake."

Conrad—a cameraman with a shock of red hair—smiled. "Thanks, Emily."

"I like the camera angle you used here," she added.

Wes, the other cameraman, stood taller. "That's my shot."

She patted his arm. "These will make great travelogues to go between the dating scenes."

"Vignettes like this are all we've really got." Brad Hammond, the show's producer and on-camera host, looked more like a surfer in his board shorts, tropical shirt and flip-flops. His bleached blond hair matched his whitened toothpaste-ad teeth. "Eating dinner in silence or discussing polo doesn't make for must-see TV."

Her face scrunched. "Please tell me you're kidding."

The collar of Luc's shirt tightened. He'd told them no respectable royal would open up on camera, but the crew hadn't listened.

"Let's just say the princess wooing lacks a certain pizzazz," Wes admitted.

Conrad nodded. "And no kissing, either."

Emily looked at the two cameramen. "You've been film-ing for a month. Surely there's been something going on."

Luc's stomach twisted. Princesses weren't going to do anything to risk their reputations unless they were willing to see this through to the end. None had wanted a second date. That meant no kissing him or touching or...

"He's kissed a few hands," Conrad said.

Wes nodded. "Escorted them by the arm."

Brad rubbed his chin. "Too bad we didn't dress them in Regency period clothing, and use a Jane Austen slant. There's a niche market for her fans."

"If you want skin and scandal, don't forget we have cell-phone video from the strip poker game," Dylan said. "One of the women left her phone behind. All we'd have to do is enhance the film."

"Let's hope she was the only person taping. Make sure that footage disappears forever." Emily's voice hardened. "All we need is for that to wind up on the Internet."

Guilt stuck in Luc's mouth like peanut butter. He shouldn't be thinking about Emily as a potential or former lover. She was here to help, and her protectiveness made him feel not so alone. Bodyguards were paid to look out for him. The crew wanted only a hit show. That left no one in his corner. No one except Emily.

"Show me the date footage." Her tone was curt, but professional. "We need to figure a way to salvage this before I leave on Tuesday."

That was only a few days from now. Luc moved closer.

Conrad typed on a keyboard. "You'd better have lots of coffee nearby or you'll fall asleep. We're talking b-o-r-i-n-g."

"Whose fault is that?"

Emily's pointed question to the crew surprised Luc. Unexpected warmth flowed through him. Few, less than a handful, had ever taken his side. The only person he could count on was his mother, but his father constrained her actions.

"Being on a reality TV show doesn't come with an instruction manual, yet you expect Luc to know what to do instinctually. He's a prince looking for a wife, not a frat boy looking to hook up for the night."

Each word she spoke in Luc's defense made him feel as if he'd found a new friend. Friends were...rare. Most others were acquaintances and hanger-ons.

She squared her shoulders. "Did he watch dating reality shows before starring in one?"

No, Luc hadn't, but he kept his mouth closed. Emily could handle this.

The crew looked at each other as if confused.

"Your silence says he didn't." Her tone reminded him of a former tutor when he hadn't studied hard enough. "Did you tell Luc what you wanted with the show?"

"Yes." Brad punctuated the word with a nod. "I told him

drama, sexual innuendoes, and hot kisses so viewers would be enticed to watch week after week."

"And what did Luc say?" she asked.

This was his cue. Luc walked across the tiled terrace. "I told him any respectable princess qualified to be my wife isn't going to open up on camera, let alone be affectionate. We're taught from birth to be private and be on-guard in front of cameras."

And most were, unless partying. Talking in front of cameras, unless for a scheduled interview or appearance, went against his nature.

"That explains the lack of interesting conversations and romance." Emily crossed her arms over her chest.

The action brought more attention to her breasts. He took a peek, then raised his gaze to her face.

"Why didn't you listen to Luc?" Emily asked Brad.

The producer shrugged. "The royalty consultant thought Luc was being difficult."

Emily's gaze narrowed in on Brad. "This was the same consultant you fired for incompetence, correct?"

"Yes, but this was before we found out she knew nothing about royals, but was one of Kendra's BFFs from college." Brad glanced at his cellphone, not the least bit apologetic. "We'd better figure out a new strategy for his date today."

See you here at bedtime tomorrow night.

It's a date.

No one would know about Luc's exchange with Emily last night. Brad must be talking about something else. "I have a date?"

A satisfied smiled formed on Emily's lips. "Yes, with Princess Brigitte of the Isle d'Etoile."

Emily amazed him, and her smile suited her pretty face better than a frown. "How did you set up a date for today when you arrived yesterday?"

"WiFi. I contacted princesses during layovers. I should hear from more soon. I'm hoping to find you a dinner partner." She motioned to him. "But right now, you need to come with me so we can figure out the best way for you to sweep Princess Brigitte off her feet."

Luc shook his head. "I know how to romance a woman."

"How?"

He thought about his most recent dates. None came to mind, only women he'd met at parties or clubs. Most, if not all, had come onto him. Zero had played hard to get. A drink, a compliment, maybe a dance but that didn't seem to be a deal breaker, and he'd be set for the night.

"So…" Emily said.

Damn. Luc didn't want to tell her he was the one pursued by women. Nor did he want to lie about not having to go to much effort or romance. "You'll see when it's time. Until then, tell me your ideas on how to woo a princess."

STANDING ON THE terrace next to Luc, Emily struggled for something to say. Random ideas swirled through her head like water disappearing down a drain. She'd expected him to tell her how he romanced women, and they would go from there, not have to come up with something from scratch.

Luc looked at her expectedly. "You do have a plan."

"I always have a plan." And she would, as soon as she had time to think. She'd never been romanced Reality TV style. Her dating life was more about convenience and companionship than romance. But she'd imagined perfect dates more than once. She would have to do the same here.

"But since this is your date, let's start with you."

He drew back. "Me?"

Emily nodded, as ideas became more concrete. "Take me to your favorite place at the villa."

"I have two."

She wanted to see both, but there wasn't time. "Which one would be best for tea?"

His mouth puckered as if he'd eaten a lemon. "Tea is not what I'd call a romantic first date."

"Anything can be romantic." She remembered helping Nick surprise Addie on her birthday with dinner on the beach. Not even wind or a bunch of navy trainees running across the sand could spoil the meal. "The right frame of mind and a thought-out setting can make all the difference."

He gave her a look. "You don't know what Princess Brigitte is thinking or what kind of date she expects."

"She suggested tea because she has another obligation tonight and is busy this weekend."

His brows furrowed. "She told you this?"

"Her secretary did. While you have tea, I'll be meeting with her to get a crash course in European royalty."

"Follow me." He led her down a path in the opposite direction from the kitchen garden. "Why are you leaving on Tuesday?"

"I have a meeting to attend on Wednesday."

"Reschedule the meeting."

His regal tone made her feel like one of his minions. "I can't. The client set the date." If she signed them, nothing would stand in the way of her promotion. Succeeding with the show would be the icing, rather a bonus in her paycheck. "It's...important."

"I need you here."

His words touched something deep within her. She liked feeling needed, but she'd rather feel like a minion with him.

"Don't worry." She climbed down a short staircase. "I'll have your calendar filled before I leave. Addie is staying. She's more than capable to handle this. Everything will be fine."

Up ahead, she saw an old clock tower that looked like something from the Renaissance time period.

Luc walked a little farther, then stopped on a secluded brick patio that was in the clock tower's shadows and surrounded by bushes and trees. "This is the spot."

"Lovely." Roses scented the air and provided splashes of color to all the green. "Perfect, actually. Wes and Conrad can hide with their cameras. That might put Princess Brigitte more at ease. Too bad there's nothing we can do about the microphone packs. Can't risk bad audio."

"You never stop working."

"Just doing my job." If she didn't, she might find herself working on more of these stupid shows in the future. Being a partner meant her boss couldn't give her these "extra" assignments. "You'd make it easier if you'd talk about the foundation, but I know that's not a possibility. Yet."

"We're not close to that being possible."

True, but she wasn't giving up on figuring out how to bring the foundation into the show.

Emily looked around, then closed her eyes.

"What are you doing?" Luc asked.

"Imagining what would make this spot more perfect." She opened her eyes. "This is a romantic setting, and I want to up that. If we arrange a small round table with two chairs, you can sit close, knee to knee, during tea."

He stepped closer to her. Heat emanated from his body. "Forced proximity."

His scent circled her head, making her feel like she'd drunk a mimosa for breakfast, not orange juice. Her mouth went dry. "Close seating sounds less calculating."

"The entire show is calculated."

"The reality in Reality TV is a misnomer."

She expected Luc to move away. Instead he came closer until he stood right next to her. "Calling it Pretend TV would turn off viewers."

"You're catching on to how this works," she said.

"Unfortunately."

The depths of his blue eyes mesmerized her. Her stomach tingled, as if a butterfly had gotten loose inside and was trying to get out. Being with Luc didn't feel quite real.

"But I'm game," he continued. "Let's go all the way with the romance. I'll give the princess a bouquet of roses."

Another idea popped into Emily's head. "No bouquet. One flower. A perfect red rose from a bud vase on the table."

"That won't look calculated?"

"A single rose is still a romantic gesture."

"You'd like that?"

"Very much so." Emily imagined Luc handing her a flower. His gaze would be intent upon hers like now. His fingers would brush across her skin. Warmth balled at the center of her chest.

"We should dance."

Luc's words brought her back from the daydream. Anticipation spurted through her. "Dance?"

"After tea, I'll ask the princess to dance."

The princess, not Emily.

Talk about feeling ridiculous thinking he meant dancing with her. She was here to work, not be romanced by the prince. She needed to tattoo the words on her forehead.

Well, in invisible ink that only she could see.

"Dancing would be very romantic," she agreed. "Dylan can figure a way to pipe in music."

"Or we could dance without it." Luc took Emily in his arms.

She stiffened. "What are you doing?"

"Seeing if there's enough space to dance." He moved her around the small patio like they were at the ball in *Cinderella*.

She tried to remain rigid and in control, to not think about being in his arms or that in her head she heard music and in her heart...

"There's room to dance." She stopped, but he continued leading her around the patio. "We can stop now."

"If I practice, this will feel more natural later."

"You're doing fine."

"Thank you." He grinned wryly. "Though I hope Princess Brigitte isn't as tense as you are. Relax."

Emily had to stay tense. If she let her guard down she might forget this was nothing more than practicing. "The princess might be nervous."

He gently rubbed Emily's shoulder blade. "If she is, I'll do this to help her relax."

Emily bit back a moan of pleasure. She fought the urge to lean into him. The man had magic fingers.

"Once I feel her loosening up, I'll compliment her dancing. Tell her she's light on her feet and moves like a ballerina."

A lump formed in Emily's throat. She knew he was making up lines, but he sounded surprisingly sincere. "Those words will make her feel special. Women like feeling that way."

"I won't stop there."

Emily shouldn't ask, but curiosity got the best of her. "What else will you say?"

"That you're beautiful." Strands of her hair sifted through his fingers. "And your golden hair is softer than silk."

"G-good." Emily forced the word out. Her voice sounded raw, almost husky. She couldn't help it, even though he was talking about Princess Brigitte.

"I'll pull her closer, watching to make sure she's okay with what I'm doing." He did, and Emily was. "Then I'll…"

She reminded herself to breathe. "What?"

Luc stopped dancing. He lowered his mouth, pressing his lips against hers before she had time to turn her head or back away.

Tender. Sweet. Oh, my.

Luc's lips caressed hers like she was precious and fragile. Surprisingly, unexpectedly…gentle.

She soaked up the taste and feel of him. Warm and male. Luc.

Somewhere a warning sounded, but she ignored it. One kiss wouldn't change anything.

He pulled her closer, pressed his mouth firmer against hers. The gentleness disappeared, replaced by hunger.

And heat. Oh, wow.

His kiss tantalized and teased. She parted her mouth, hoping he'd take the invitation. He did. Tongues mingled, danced, explored.

She combed her fingers through his hair, the way he had hers. Her insides tightened, a need suddenly growing, wanting…more.

He pulled her even closer, and she arched, pressing against him. So tall, so strong.

A bird chirped. In her imagination or real, she didn't know. Nor did she care. His kiss was real. That was enough for her.

He moved his lips away from her mouth and showered kisses along her jawline to her ear. She melted into him. Then tingles exploded. Pleasurable sensations cascaded through her.

Oh, yes.

Emily's control slipped. She wanted more kisses, more Luc…

Oh, no. What was she doing? She was here to find him a bride. Not kiss him herself.

She tore away from him. "Stop."

"We're just practicing."

Maybe he was, but her lips throbbed. Her body burned. The kiss had been real to her. "We've practiced enough."

"Maybe you have, but I'm thinking we might need a dress rehearsal. Sans cameras, of course." He reached for Emily.

She leaned away so his hand found only air. "You have this down."

The guy was a master kisser. Experienced. She'd never been kissed so thoroughly in her life. She doubted she'd ever be kissed as well again. Whatever princess landed him would be living a fairy tale.

Too bad, she wasn't royalty, but she'd seen a genealogy chart. No blueblood on either sides of her family. "If you get Princess Brigitte to the kissing part, you'll be set."

"Thanks, perhaps if we keep practicing…"

The way his voice trailed off told Emily he was waiting for her answer. Her lips screamed yes! They wanted more kisses.

A part of Emily did, too. A big part if she were being honest with herself. But that wasn't the part of her ruled by logic or common sense.

"No, we're finished kissing."

Even if her lips wanted more kisses. She had a job to do, one she couldn't accomplish if she were kissing Luc. And liking his kiss. Make that kisses.

She needed to focus on the show, on her dream of being promoted. "If you're kissing me that means you're not kissing any princesses."

"It was one kiss."

She deflated like a balloon. Even if she'd told herself the same thing when his lips touched hers. But Luc had redefined the word kiss. "I know that."

He raised a brow. "Really?"

Cocky ass. Now he'd just ruined the moment. Good, because she couldn't afford any more moments with him. "Yes, so don't act all vain. Women don't like that."

"What do they like?"

"Men being themselves and honest. Some flowers, dancing, and kisses won't hurt. Most importantly, make her feel as if she's the only woman in your world."

A charming grin spread across his face and reached his eyes. "I can do that."

Her heart bumped. "Yes, you can."

And knowing that bugged the hell out of Emily.

THAT AFTERNOON, LUC sat across from Princess Brigitte at the small table Emily had set up complete with linen cloth, china tea service, and a crystal bud vase with one perfect red rose. Romantic, yes. Intimate, however, might be a misnomer. Crowded was a better adjective. If his hands weren't bumping into the princess, then his knees were. Fortunately Brigitte didn't seem to mind.

Too bad he wished another woman were sitting across from him instead. Emily had surprised him once again. This time with a kiss that seared his lips and made him want another.

Made him want…

"Each dish has been delightful." Brigitte stared over the rim of her teacup. "Please pass on my compliments to the chef."

"I will." He forced himself to concentrate on the lovely princess. "The chef used recipes from Alvernia for the desserts."

"Your country is known for its delicious pastries."

"And yours for its beautiful royal family."

Brigitte tilted her head in acknowledgement of his compliment. The ends of her long brown hair fell mid-back. Perfectly applied makeup accentuated her features. Her light blue short-sleeved dress was made for an outing such as this. She was exactly the type of wife he was looking for, one that would make a lovely princess bride and please his parents.

So why wasn't he feeling any sort of attraction? And why did he wish Emily were out here instead of inside the villa with Brigitte's secretary.

Brigitte glanced around until her gaze came to a rose bush. "This is a lovely spot."

"One of my favorites at the villa. Though I'd never considered having tea here until today." He raised his teacup, a silent toast to Emily. "Thank you for joining me."

Brigitte's closed mouth, polite-looking smile didn't tell Luc much. But this date had gone better than any during the past month. Not bad given Emily had been here less than twenty-four hours. But he needed to concentrate on the woman sitting across from him. She could be the solution to his problem—the way for him to remain a member of the royal family and keep his foundation going.

"Your invitation surprised me." Brigitte seemed relaxed, even though cameras were filming through the bushes. Their earlier conversations hadn't been only about the weather and polo, but growing up royal, attending university, and their love of gelato. "I thought I'd been left off your list."

Luc had never seen the first list or the new one for that matter. But he remembered what Emily said about making a woman feel special.

He took the rose from the bud vase, dried the water from the stem with his napkin, and handed the flower to Brigitte.

Her lips formed a perfect o, then spread into an open-mouthed smile. Her first during the tea.

"The original list of names was from the former consultant with the show," he admitted. "I'm sorry for the oversight. I'm fortunate my new list includes you. I'm enjoying our time together."

Luc spoke the truth. He only wished there was a spark between them, something to make him take Brigitte in his arms, dance with no music playing, and kiss her the way he had with Emily.

Brigitte raised the rose to her nose and sniffed. "Apology accepted. I'm enjoying myself. This is not what I expected."

"What was that?"

"A Bacchanalian orgy of sorts."

Emily was right about his reputation. "I hope you're not disappointed."

"Perhaps a little." Amusement twinkled in Brigette's brown eyes. She stood. "I'm only sorry I can't stay longer, but I have an engagement tonight."

Luc rose. "Duty above all else."

"We do what we must. And sometimes, like this afternoon, that turns out better than expected."

She must have been forced to come today.

"Thank you for joining me." He extended his arm to escort her up the path to the villa. This was his chance to ask for a second date. He'd been turned down every time before. "Perhaps you will have time in your busy schedule to visit again."

She studied him. Not as a princess would, but as a shrewd, calculating lawyer might. "How long do you have until your engagement presentation?"

Not nearly long enough. "Two weeks."

Brigitte stepped towards him, rose up on her toes, and kissed him on the lips. Unexpected, but pleasant. No burst of heat or fireworks. Maybe next time?

She drew back, then smelled the rose again. "I'd be happy to visit again. Early next week?"

"I'd like that very much." Luc would, given what was at stake.

"Then it's a date."

His second. And no mention of the foundation needed. He should be thrilled and want to celebrate. But all he could think about was how much better he liked Emily's kiss than Brigitte's.

Chapter Six

E MILY SAT IN the villa's library at a large mahogany desk. Ornate gilded bookshelves filled with hardcovers, many first editions, lined the walls. The smells of the pages and bindings were stronger than the two antique chairs in front of the fireplace and a smaller writing table on the far wall.

She clicked *yes* in the *second date* column of her database. Finding a princess who wanted to go out with him again was what Luc needed, except…

She touched her lips. No more throbbing or tingles, only the memory of Luc's kiss from a couple hours ago. But a longing for more kept growing. Anticipation of spending more time with him prickled like pins and needles. She didn't believe in true love's kiss, but she wanted to kiss him again.

Partner. Partner. Partner.

The word became a mantra to help her forget Luc's toe-curling kiss—well, practice one—and focus on finding him a bride.

"The tea went well."

She looked up from her laptop to see Luc standing on the other side of the desk with a smile on his face. He wore a blue suit, blue shirt, and checked blue tie. His hands were behind his back.

"Brad told me." She hit save, then closed her laptop. "Congratulations."

He brought his arms forward. He held a pink rose in one hand and a chocolate bar in the other. "Thanks for your help."

A weight pressed down on her chest making breathing difficult. She wasn't used to receiving gifts. Not from a man, rather a client, let alone a prince.

Emily accepted his offerings with shaky hands. "You didn't have to do this. I'm just—"

"Doing your job," Luc finished for her. "I wanted to show my gratitude. My…appreciation."

She smiled, feeling tingly all over. "Can't get much better than flowers and Swiss chocolate. Thanks."

"Since Nick won't allow me to leave the grounds, I had to get creative. The rose is from the flower garden, and I raided the chef's pantry. With permission, of course."

Emily sniffed the rose. Sweet. "Very thoughtful of you."

And so unexpected. He didn't seem like the same man from yesterday morning who'd been hungover and trying to get a reaction from her by tossing back the sheet. Had she misjudged him or was he trying to play her?

Either way, she couldn't lose her head over his gifts or crush like a teenager because of a hot kiss. Nothing could stand in the way of her getting the job done.

"I have Princess Brigitte's cell number." Emily handed him a Post-It note. "Send her a text in the next day or two. Just don't go overboard."

"Do I look like a stalker?"

He looked like a dream come true. She swallowed around the tiara-sized lump in her throat. "No, but desperate times…"

"With you here, I'm no longer feeling as desperate. I have a second date."

"A dinner date tonight also."

His forehead creased. "Two dates in one day?"

"Making up for lost time. We don't have nearly enough film to make a show." She glanced at another note on the desk. "Princess Dimitra of Crystopolas and Eros Isle will be arriving at eight."

"Never met her."

"She knows who you are." Emily had spoken to the princess herself. "Let's make the evening unforgettable."

"Sounds good, but first I want to show you my other favorite spot here at the villa. The romantic possibilities are endless there. Might give us some ideas."

His suggestive grin lit a spark deep inside her. If this kept up, she was going to need to carry a fire extinguisher.

Partner. Partner. Partner.

The mantra didn't help her much. Especially gazing into Luc's killer baby blues. She looked away. Stood.

"I'd love to see the spot. Maybe we can use it for your date tonight."

"Or for another princess if you have more dates lined up for me."

"Not yet, but I'm working on it."

She was giving royal social secretaries and assistants the hard sell. Some didn't buy her the-prince-has-a-hidden-side-no-one-knows-about spiel, but a few had. That was all he needed. The sooner Luc found his bride, the better for Dream Big Alvernia and all involved.

Especially her, who was learning first hand just how irresistible Prince Luc was. And how dangerous too.

BEES BUZZED AROUND the potted flowers on the terrace, but Luc wasn't worried about being stung. He was more concerned about Emily realizing tonight's sunset was at seven-thirty, half an hour before Princess Dimitra's arrival. But he wanted alone time with Emily without the film crew, his bodyguard, and her assistant lingering nearby. The secluded area surrounded by trees and shrubbery where a small lawn led to the beach seemed perfect.

"So where's your spot?" she asked.

Emily's hair smelled like flowers. Shampoo or perfume?

He couldn't tell the difference.

"Luc?"

"Sorry." He sounded distracted, which he was. "It's by the lake."

"I haven't been down there yet."

"The stairs going down to the lake are steep." He reached for her hand. "I don't want you to fall."

She eyed their hands warily. "Sounds more like a line."

Birds chirped. The breeze lifted the ends of her hair.

"It's not." He didn't let go. Her skin was soft and smooth and warm against his. "I thought women liked gentlemen."

She seemed to relax. "Are manners something you're taught?"

"Etiquette lessons began as soon as I could speak." The path narrowed. He walked a step ahead of her. "Even now, Mrs. Renault's directions swirl through my head each time I'm in a social situation where I could make a *faux pas* as she liked to call them. Her gravelly old voice annoyed me when I was a kid. Still does."

Emily laughed. "Growing up in a palace must be so different to being raised in a beach town."

He led her down the steps. "Where was that?"

"Coronado, California."

He'd stayed at the Hotel del Coronado during a visit to the San Diego area when he was nineteen. He'd been surprised to learn the US didn't have topless beaches like

France's Cote d'Azur. "A nice town."

"Great place to grow up. That's where I met Addie and Nick. We were all in school together."

"Is your family still there?"

Emily's smiled disappeared. "No. I live in San Diego now. My mom moved away. My dad...he did, too."

"Do you see them much?"

"No, but that's okay. I'm busy with work."

Luc wondered if she was trying to convince him or herself. "I don't see my family that often."

Her gaze narrowed. "Don't you live at the palace?"

"Officially, yes." He lowered his voice as if letting her in on a secret. He was. "Unofficially, I have my own place."

Water cascaded down a three-tiered fountain to their left.

Emily slowed her pace. "Every time I take a walk, I find something new about this place."

Below them on the lake, boaters and water skiers enjoyed the spring sunshine. He enjoyed the slow pace of life here. He could take his time and get to know Emily better.

Luc squeezed her hand. "That's how I feel whenever I spend time with you."

Her gaze met his. She dragged her teeth across her lower lip.

"Not much to learn." She picked up her pace as if eager to get to their destination...or running away. "Work is my life."

"Work is important to you, but it's not everything.

You're a good friend according to Nick and Addie. A daughter too."

She shrugged, but the last thing she looked was indifferent. "Friend, yes, but daughter, not so much. My family's the definition of dysfunctional."

"I thought that title belonged to my family," he half-joked.

"Guess there are lots of us who feel that way."

Luc nodded. "My mother wanted another daughter. My father didn't want more children. I was a disappointment to both my parents as soon as I arrived."

"That must have sucked."

Emily's way with words brought a smile to his face. He nodded. "I was so much younger than my siblings; we were never really brothers and sisters. They were too busy to deal with me, so I was more like an only child."

He wanted to say more, but honor and duty kept him quiet.

"I was an only child." Emily stared at the lake. "My mom married my dad a week after she graduated college. Turns out he was a serial cheater, but she was afraid to divorce him. She didn't think she could get a job and feared losing the house in Coronado. So instead, she lost herself in alcohol to cope with her horrible marriage."

No wonder Emily had no sympathy for his hangover yesterday. Her wanting chocolate, not champagne, made more sense now.

He squeezed her hand again. "Are your parents divorced now?"

She nodded. "When I was ten, my father left us for a younger woman who was pregnant."

"Us?"

"After he moved out, he didn't want visitation rights. I reminded my dad of my mother, so I wasn't welcome in his new family. On my eleventh birthday, he sent me Miss Mousie. That was the last time I heard from him. Probably silly to hold onto a stuffed animal all these years."

"Not silly. The cat is your part of him even if he's no longer in your life." Luc's heart ached for Emily. His father wouldn't win any parenting awards, but the king had provided a place to live, an allowance, and an education when Luc was growing up. Everything changed once he became an adult. But to be a kid...

He wanted to hug her, but rubbed his thumb against her hand instead. "A father should never abandon his child. I'm sorry yours did. That must have been difficult on you."

"Harder on my mom." Emily's tone was more resigned than hurt. "She wasted so much time holding on to a bad marriage because she didn't know how we'd survive without my dad paying the bills. That taught me to take care of myself so I'll never find myself in the same situation."

No wonder Emily worked so hard. His respect for her grew. "You're a strong woman."

"Thanks, but I must also be jet lagged." Emily shook her

head. "I can't believe I'm telling you all this. It's not something I talk about to anyone."

"I'm glad you told me."

"I don't want pity."

"You'll get none from me." He wanted to kiss the sadness in her eyes away, but he didn't want to take advantage of her vulnerability. Telling him about her parents had to have taken a leap of trust. His turn. "Do you know why I'm doing this show?"

"Your father."

"Yes." On the lake below, a water skier fell. That was how Luc felt, out of control, about to crash and burn if he hit the wake wrong. But he wanted Emily to know he understood. "The king, my father, gave me an ultimatum. If I don't present a fiancée at the palace in two weeks, I will be stripped of my title and my allowance. I will be disowned."

Her face paled. "He can do that?"

"The king can do whatever he pleases. Not even my mother has been able to change his mind." Luc took a deep breath. Telling someone else took a weight off his shoulders. "The worst part of being disowned is not being able to run the foundation the way I have been. My title gives me access to people and places for my fundraising events. Donations help, but my allowance funds the foundation. Without that…"

"Oh, Luc." Emily stroked his shoulder with her free hand. "I'm so sorry you're having to go through this."

Her compassion touched his heart. "It is what it is. I'm resigned to any marriage so long as my father approves. That's the only way to keep the foundation running."

"Then it's good you have me." The words flew from her mouth faster than the *profiteroles* had disappeared from the buffet lunch earlier. Her usual confidence bubbled over making him smile. "I'll do everything within my power to find you a bride before I have to leave. I'll download every peerage list, cross-reference them, and see if there's any nobility we haven't contacted. If I could use the foundation—"

"Still off limits."

She lowered her hand from his arm and bit her lip.

He could imagine what she was thinking. "You think I'm more stupid."

"Stubborn, too."

"Anything else?"

"Yes, but we have an over-the-top romantic date to plan. And not much time."

"You're amazing."

"I'm exactly what you need right now." Emily smiled like a ray of sunshine breaking through overcast skies. "No worries, okay? By the time we're finished, Princess Dimitra won't know what hit her."

That was how Luc felt about Emily. She'd blasted into his life like a high speed Italo train, and he had the feeling he'd never be the same.

THAT EVENING ON the villa's pool terrace, Emily fixed a crooked flower on the table's centerpiece. Torches and candles flickered and reflected in the water. Miniature white lights glowed. Soft music played from outside speakers. Additional flowerpots had been moved from around the villa and set around the edges of the swimming pool to make the setting for Luc's dinner with Princess Dimitra more romantic. Underwater lighting added to the inviting atmosphere. Perhaps Luc and his date would want to swim after they ate.

"Everything looks wonderful." Luc looked like a groom in his tuxedo. "You outdid yourself."

His compliment pleased Emily. "The staff helped. Addie strung the miniature white lights."

"A whimsical touch."

"If you like that sort of thing."

"You don't?"

The lights made Emily think of a fairy tale or amusement park. "I'm practical."

That meant even though she was embarrassed for opening up the way she had about her parents, she was also relieved knowing what was at stake for Luc. Failure had never been an option, but she felt more urgency knowing about the king's ultimatum.

"Yet you plan romantic dates," Luc said.

"I'm here to help."

She spoke the words as much for his benefit as hers. He

was a client, nothing else. So what if the secluded spot he'd taken her to this afternoon was the perfect setting for another kiss? His kisses weren't meant for her.

"Is your microphone on?" she asked.

"Not yet." He motioned to the pack he wore at his waist. "Nick taught me how to turn it off and on."

"Turn it on." The words came out like a captain's order. She softened her voice. "The princess will be here any minute."

"Nervous?"

"No." Emily straightened another flower. "I want tonight to go well for you."

"Look at this table, the flowers, the lights, the pool, and me." A charming smile spread to his eyes. "What could go wrong?"

"Nothing. You make James Bond look like he shops at a thrift store and cuts his own hair."

Luc gave a mock bow. "I aim to please."

If only he could please her... Emily swallowed a sigh.

The villa's butler, a man in his fifties named Aldo, stood at the doorway to the drawing room. He cleared his throat. "Her Royal Highness Princess Dimitra of Crystopolas and Eros Isle."

"I'm going to slip into the darkness." Emily headed into the pool cabana where the crew had set up their equipment. The location gave her a perfect view of the terrace. She couldn't wait to see Luc on a date. She'd been speaking with

Princess Brigitte's secretary and missed watching the tea.

"Hey," she whispered to Dylan. "Ready?"

"All set." His left headphone was off his ear. "I've got twenty bucks riding on this princess kissing him longer than the first one did."

Emily's stomach did a somersault. "Brigitte kissed Luc?"

"Right on the lips. She looked like she wanted another one, but she had to leave."

Emily knew how the princess must have felt wanting more. Except Brigitte's kiss hadn't been for practice. Hers had meant something. The thought left Emily feeling uneasy. A stupid reaction when her goal was to find Luc a wife.

"Here comes the princess." Dylan kept his voice low. "Whoa, baby. Look at that rack. Talk about hot. Luc will have to tell us if she's a natural blonde."

"Do your job. And let Luc do his."

Dylan shook his head. "If the prince doesn't propose to this one, there's something wrong with him. The woman is sexy as hell. Look at that ass."

Emily wanted to see what the fuss was about.

Talk about gorgeous. The princess had more curves than Lombard Street in San Francisco. While Brigitte looked like a quintessential princess from the pages of a magazine, Dimitra could have been mistaken for an escort or stripper.

She crossed the tiled terrace in four-inch heels and a scandalously short skirt. If Emily's eyes weren't deceiving her, the princess wore red lace panties. Sexy blonde curls bounced. The princess's ample breasts appeared ready to break out of her corset top at any second.

"Come on wardrobe malfunction," Dylan muttered.

Luc's mouth dropped open. He stared at Dimitra like she was a mountain spring and he was dehydrated and needed water. No matter that he stood in front of a swimming pool. That wouldn't quench his thirst.

Not that Emily blamed him. The princess was dressed for a night of seduction and sex, not a romantic dinner date with a potential spouse.

Luc met her halfway, as if he didn't want to wait two more minutes to let her come to him.

Emily wanted to throw up. A reaction she'd never experienced with a client. Still she wanted to know what's going on. "Give me a set of earphones."

Dylan did.

She heard Luc swallow. The man was definitely attracted. Likely turned on.

He bowed. "Good evening, Your Highness."

"Well, hello to you, sir." Dimitra's voice was sensual-husky. "May we drop protocol so I can call you Luc?"

The princess purred his name.

"Feel free to call me whatever you'd like." He escorted her to the table-for-two positioned near where water from the hot tub cascaded down steps into the main pool. He handed her a flute of champagne that had been poured minutes ago.

She took the glass. "I'd like you to call me what you did when we met on New Year's Eve."

"We met in Paris?"

The woman sucked in a breath. "Aspen."

"I was in Paris that night." He gave her the once-over, his eyes filled with desire. "Trust me, I'd remember meeting you."

"I don't know why you won't admit you were in Aspen." Her painted and glossed lips pursed into an enormous pout. "Spending New Year's Eve with you was the best night of my life. You agreed we were soulmates, but then I never heard from you again. I texted, called. Nothing. I've been heartbroken for over three months."

No one could deny the emotion behind the woman's words. Her voice cracked more than once.

Emily looked at Dylan. "I've got a bad feeling about this."

"Don't. This is pure rating's gold. A psycho princess is exactly what the show needed."

"Not psycho. Heartbroken."

Dylan shook his head. "Only if she's telling the truth."

Emily couldn't tell who the victim was, but she knew the prince was as experienced breaking hearts as he was kissing.

Luc raised his hands, palms out, in a gesture of surrender. "I never received your calls or texts. I swear. It wasn't in Aspen. We've never met."

Dimitra's eyes hardened. The look sent chills down Emily's spine. "Where's Nick?"

"He should be around here somewhere."

Emily sent him a 911 text.

Dimitra raised her champagne glass, then took a sip. "I bet you say that to all the women whose hearts you shatter."

Luc shook his head. "No, I—"

She tossed the remaining contents of her flute at him.

He jerked back, only steps away from the pool's edge. Liquid ran down his nose, cheeks, and chin.

"Psycho," Dylan said, sounding like he was enjoying this. "Bet she's crazy in bed."

Luc blinked, wiped his face. He took half a step back, closer to the edge of the water. "I'm telling the truth."

"Liar." The woman's eyes glassed over. "You can't treat women like this."

She pushed Luc. He fell backward. His arms stretched out, but he was too close to the edge to balance himself. He fell into the pool. Water splashed. Dimitra gave a triumphant cheer.

Oh, no. Before Emily could take off the headset, Nick ran onto the terrace and subdued Dimitra, who struggled to get away.

"Are you okay, sir?" Nick asked.

Luc brushed back his wet hair. He climbed out of the pool. "Fine."

"Wait a minute." Dimitra took a closer look. "You didn't

have a scar beneath your eye in Aspen."

"I've had the scar since I was fifteen. An unfortunate accident with an ice axe while climbing." Water dripped from his hair and tuxedo. "Whatever you believe, I wasn't in Aspen."

Dimitra stared up at him. Her mouth gaped. "You're taller. Younger. More handsome too."

"Let her go," he ordered Nick.

"Thank you." She adjusted her skirt. "I suppose it's a little late for an apology, and I should go."

Please tell her to go, Emily thought.

"Let her stay," Dylan said.

"That will be best under the circumstances," Luc said in that regal tone of his.

"Too bad." Dimitra's gaze raked over him. "Bet you'd be better in bed than your namesake."

"Is it scary that I'm turned on right now?" Dylan whispered.

"Yes," Emily said without a missing a beat.

Luc looked more frightened than flattered. She wanted to give the guy a hug for bringing Princess Dimitra into his life.

"I apologize, Your Highness." Dimitra turned, then strutted out of the room, followed closely by Nick.

Emily took a step out of the cabana, but Dylan stopped her. "We're still filming."

Luc removed his tuxedo jacket. Water poured from the

sleeves. His white dress shirt was plastered to his chest, leaving nothing to the imagination.

Not that she hadn't seen him before, but the wet, see-through fabric pressed against his skin, showed off his chest and abs. Talk about sexy.

Nick returned with towels. "I shouldn't have left you alone."

"Not your fault. Hers, either." Luc dried himself. "She believed I was in Aspen with her. I'm sure someone was."

"Your doppelgänger?"

Luc hesitated, wiped his face with a towel. "Maybe. Who knows? Some guy could have been feeding her a line."

Emily could tell by the two-second hesitation that Luc knew more than he was saying.

"I'm going to shower, then I'll be back for dinner. No reason to let the chef's cooking go to waste." Luc glanced around. "Everyone is welcome to join me. Emily?"

She was surprised he knew she was there. She peeked out of the cabana. "Sure. That's the least I can do after setting up this dating disaster."

"No one knew that Dimitra was here to rekindle a romance," Luc said.

"We need to be more careful." Nick cleaned up the towels. "I'm going to run background checks on Luc's future dates."

Emily agreed something more needed to be done to ensure Luc's safety. "I'll get you the information you need."

"Be back shortly." Luc walked into the villa.

Nick looked at Emily. "Do you think the woman is crazy or she really thought Luc was in Aspen?"

"I don't know, but I'm going to find out right now."

And not only for her sake.

THIRTY MINUTES LATER, Luc sat across from Emily on the terrace. He wasn't disappointed how his date had ended, though he'd rather not have been pushed into the pool. Still, having dinner with Emily was worth it.

A server went to refill Luc's wine glass. He cut him off once he saw Emily's glass was still full. "No more."

"Have another glass," Emily said. "I don't mind."

But Luc did. "One glass is enough."

"After the night you had?"

He wanted her to feel comfortable around him. He motioned the man away. "Brad said a drama princess is exactly what the show needed. The crew is thrilled with the footage."

"Let's hope she's the only crazy one."

"I know I'm in good hands." Luc wished he could be touching those hands right now. He took another bite of halibut instead.

"Dimitra seemed certain she was with you in Aspen."

Luc took another bite so he didn't have to reply.

"I did an Internet search while you showered," Emily

continued. "Your older brothers and their families were in Aspen over New Year's."

Damn. Luc wiped his mouth. "They were?"

"Yes." She set her fork on her plate. "I noticed something else. You look like a younger, taller version of the crown prince. Just as Princess Dimitra said."

His stomach knotted. He reached for his wine glass only to remember it was empty. "She also said I was more handsome."

"Princess Dimitra thought she'd been with you because Prince Bernard used your name instead of his."

It wasn't a question. "Emily—"

"That's what you meant about not being in drug rehab." Her lips parted, the gears in her brain turning like crazy. "It wasn't you, but him. Your parents lied."

Luc took a breath, then another. "Please. You can't say anything. Bernard's the next king of Alvernia. The people cannot lose confidence in him and the monarchy."

"Someone with addiction issues and who cheats on his wife doesn't sound like he'll be a noble ruler."

"Bernard's first in line to the throne." Luc wanted her to understand. "That's all that matters."

"No, you matter."

"Thank you."

"I'm serious." She spoke louder. "You've bought into what people think of you. Accepting their views of you. People think you're—"

"There are expectations I must live up to."

"Live up to your own. No one else's expectations matter."

"I do what I must for my family and country. Even if it means being my brother's scapegoat."

"It's not fair. What happens after you marry? Will you continue to take the fall for Bernard's indiscretions?"

"No. That wouldn't be fair to my wife. Even my father agrees. He said Bernard will behave or else."

Luc had no idea what his father meant by *or else*.

She toyed with her napkin.

Luc reached across the table and touched her forearm. If he held her hand, he might not want to let go.

"No one's cared enough to figure out what's going on. It means..." Everything. "...a lot that you did."

Her gaze met his. "I hate to say this, but it's almost as if your father has set you up to fail."

"He has." Once again, her insight surprised him. "That is why I must succeed. With your help, I will."

A thoughtful expression formed on Emily's face. "I know your foundation is off-limits, but perhaps you could visit a hospital or school during your second dates? Something to show that side of your personality to the princesses."

"You're not going to give up."

"I believe this will make a difference in your search."

"Have you talked to Nick about this?"

"I wanted to see what you thought first."

"If Nick agrees, then I'll go."

"Nick agrees," a familiar voice said from the shadows.

"There's your answer." Luc laughed.

She looked around. "I didn't realize Nick was here."

"My bodyguard is always lurking. He's often out of my sight, but I'm rarely out of his." Thank goodness for non-disclosure agreements.

Emily's eyes twinkled. "You won't regret this."

"If I do, you'll have to make it up to me."

"What do you have in mind?" she asked.

He pictured a blanket on the sand, her lips against his. "Oh, I have a few ideas."

Chapter Seven

TWO DAYS LATER, Emily was running on fumes. She sat at the desk in the library trying to do four things at once. Thank goodness for coffee or she'd be passed out in the chair.

No television viewer wanted to watch the same date twice. Trying to come up with different romantic dates at the villa stretched her creativity to the limit.

Only two first dates remained. She hoped these went well. Not all had. Dimitra's was the worst, but others with an addicted texter from Meinstin and an annoying giggler from Herzenslust had been busts. A good thing brunch with Princess Jemma, an astrophysicist from Melia and dessert with Princess Sophie, a social worker from Alistonia, made up for the bad dates.

A short list of second date candidates was forming. So were ideas to showcase Luc's positive traits to those women.

Addie set a file on her desk. "Visits to the hospital as well as a local school are arranged. But do you really want to rent a litter of puppies for an afternoon?"

"I doubt any mother would loan us her kids for a few hours, so puppies will have to do."

"The breeder wants to supervise."

"That's fine as long as they sign an NDA."

"He also wants his kennel's name listed on the credits."

"Ask Brad. He's the producer so needs to sign off on that."

Addie scribbled notes on a pad of paper. "You should take off an hour or two. I've enjoyed sightseeing, but it would be more fun if I wasn't alone."

"Maybe before I leave."

"That means no." Addie gave her a curious look. "I bet your answer would be different if Luc asked you to go."

"What are you talking about?"

"The two of you seem chummy."

"We're…coworkers." Saying the word felt wrong. But Emily didn't know how else to describe them. "Friends."

That sounded a little better.

"The way he looks at you is not friendly. He's downright territorial. And the way you two keep disappearing to plan dates. Makes me wonder what's really going on. Nick's not saying a word when I ask."

Good for Nick. Emily scanned the papers in Addie's file. "The newlywed in you views everything through romantic colored lenses. Nothing is going on."

Unfortunately. Correction. Fortunately.

"Positive?" Addie wanted everyone to have a happily ever after.

"Yes."

"Too bad. The two of you make a cute couple."

Emily's pulse spurted. "Even if we did, which we don't, I'm not royalty. Besides I'm not interested in dating anyone, let alone a crush-worthy prince."

"So you have a crush." Addie's brows wriggled.

"Maybe a little one."

Addie beamed. "That's more than I thought you'd admit."

"Well, keep the news to yourself, okay? I have a job to do, and I need the guys to see me as a taskmaster. Not a giggling, blushing school girl."

Addie rubbed her hands together. "Oh, I'd love to see you act that way. Just once."

"Not. Going. To. Happen."

"Maybe not here, but someday…"

Emily shooed her friend away. "See if the chef's ready to go shopping."

"Going, but I'm living proof, you never know what will happen."

Emily's lips tingled from the memory of Luc's kiss by the clock tower. That had been unexpected. "Very true."

But one kiss didn't mean anything, even if she wouldn't be forgetting that kiss for a very long time.

IN THE POOL cabana, Luc found the crew reviewing footage, but no sign of Emily. That was strange. If anything, her schedule was predictable. He could count on her being where she needed to be. Luc appreciated that about her.

Too bad she had to leave on Tuesday. Because she'd found him dates, he told himself.

"Has anyone seen Emily?" he asked the crew.

"She's out with the chef." Dylan worked on one of the microphone packs. "They've come up with a special menu for your date tonight."

Another one? Luc couldn't keep track of the princesses coming in and out of the villa. "Emily doesn't cook."

"Not cooking is different from knowing how to cook but choosing not to," Brad said in an all-too-knowing voice. "Emily knows her way around the kitchen. And a few other places."

The producer's words poked like a knife. Luc didn't like that.

"The chef is cooking a seven-course meal combining dishes from Alvernia and Mariposa," Conrad said.

The back of the hair on Luc's neck stiffened. "Mariposa?"

Conrad nodded. "That's where Princess Marguerite is from."

"Mariposa means butterfly in Spanish." Wes smiled smugly. "Haven't forgotten everything I learned in high school."

A volcano-worthy headache erupted behind Luc's temples. He rubbed his forehead.

Brad touched Luc's shoulder. "Hey, you don't look so good. Are you sick?"

"I have a case of early regrets."

"Is this princess ugly or something?" Dylan asked.

"No." Luc tried to remember the last time he'd seen Marguerite. Skiing in Klosters, perhaps? They'd never been formally introduced. "She's quite beautiful."

"Then what's the problem?" Wes's brows furrowed. "Seriously, dude, you need to watch episodes of *The Bachelor*. You're the only one who's been in the pool. The hot tub hasn't been used. You're totally blowing what you could get away with here."

"I'm not trying to get away with anything. I need to find a wife." Outrageous stories about Marguerite had made the rounds at his most recent fundraisers. "But a woman who prefers to be addressed by the name Princess Butterfly may not be the right choice."

Luc trusted Emily, more than he'd trusted anyone in a long while, but this dinner had disaster written all over it. He hoped he wasn't the one getting wet again.

THAT EVENING, EMILY rechecked the formal dining room. A freshly pressed linen cloth covered the left end of the long table. The two place settings had napkins folded in the shape of a butterfly, courtesy of Addie and a YouTube video. Fresh cut flowers from one of the gardens filled a crystal vase. The candelabra would be lit soon.

Everything was perfect except for…

Luc.

He looked so…princely in his dark gray suit, starched white shirt and solid red tie. He wore a lapel pin with his family crest. His shoulder length hair added a dash of sexy to his classic style. But he kept pacing, circling the table that seated twenty-four.

Emily hadn't expected him to be nervous. Not after his other first dates. "You okay?"

He nodded once.

"You look great. But if you don't stop brooding, you're going to steal the title of Mr. Darcy away from Nick."

Lines formed on either side of Luc's mouth like cracks in granite. "You should have canceled the date when I texted you."

"Princess Marguerite was already on her way to Lake Como." Emily studied him. The guy seemed fidgety. "Why don't you want to have dinner with her?"

He shrugged.

"Marguerite can't wait to meet you. The least you can do is try to enjoy yourself."

"Marguerite is…eccentric. I've heard—"

"Wait a minute." Emily blocked his path so he couldn't

pace. "You don't want people to believe gossip about you, but you're willing to judge Marguerite on hearsay?"

"The stories are bizarre. The royal family has standards."

"Marguerite is the middle daughter of Mariposa's king. She was educated in the United States, does charity work, and is pretty."

Luc's gaze jerked up. "You saw her picture."

"In a peerage registry from a couple years ago."

His mouth twisted. "A lot can change in a couple of years."

"What are you afraid of?" Emily asked.

He raised his chin. "Nothing."

She didn't believe him. "Marguerite is traveling here to spend time with you, allowing her visit to be filmed for a television show, and deserves to be treated with respect."

"You sound like a queen."

"More like a Dowager Countess." Emily smiled, hoping he'd relax. "I stream *Downton Abbey* if I need a break."

That brought a smile to his face.

Emily straightened Luc's tie. "Marguerite has a reputation of being somewhat of a wild child. I thought that might give you something in common given your penchant for partying."

"You put thought into this."

The other princesses who had agreed to second dates seemed more proper and a little—dare she say—boring. Luc needed someone with the same vitality and zest for fun. "I've tried."

"I'll give Marguerite my full attention and be on my best behavior."

"Now let's not go overboard," Emily joked.

Another smile appeared. "I'll stop complaining."

"Good. I feel confident she's a good choice for you."

Mischief gleamed in his eyes. "Care to put a wager on it?"

"You mean a bet?"

"Yes. If Marguerite turns out to be like any other European princess, you win, but if she's at all…different, then I win."

"What's at stake?"

"Winner names the prize."

Tempting, especially if he meant… "Anything?"

"You're thinking about the foundation."

"Of course, I am."

"The foundation is included." His tone challenged her. "Are you game?"

Emily wasn't a gambler. She preferred betting only when the odds were in her favor. They were tonight. And once she could show the princess Luc's work with his foundation, she'd be able to help him plan a proposal before she left on Tuesday.

"You've got yourself a bet, but you realize I'm going to win," she said. "And you can't back down when I do."

"The same goes if I win."

"The princess's limousine's here." Dressed in white and wearing an earpiece, Brad peered into the dining room. "Get ready."

Emily's nerve endings tingled with excitement. She walked to the drawing room where introductions would take place.

Luc was at her side. His smile wavered.

She longed to reach out and give him a sign of support. He needed another princess or two to agree to a second date to up his odds of finding a fiancée.

So what if she would rather be having dinner with Luc tonight? Or the thought of his date with yet another princess left her feeling unsettled?

Emily straightened her black skirt and smoothed her white blouse. She couldn't wait to see what the princess wore.

Luc touched her shoulder.

She jumped. "What?"

"You're the one who's nervous."

"I'm excited to see how wonderful this works out. And win the bet."

"One day your confidence is going to get you into trouble."

She laughed. "Addie's said the same thing."

"For being so confident, you're tense." He squeezed Emily's shoulders, kneading the tight muscles.

The tension seeped out. "You're good at this."

"I have many skills." His tone was playful and suggestive. He leaned closer, his breath against her neck. "And a few not so hidden ones."

A chill ran the length of her spine. Goosebumps formed on her arms. "I'm getting an idea about your…talents."

"Happy to show you more."

If only… Her heart pounded in her throat. "Save it for Princess Marguerite."

"Dinner dates are my specialty."

She thought about her first night at the villa. "Especially dessert."

He continued massaging. "I can bring you cookies and milk later. We'll eat while you recite lines of Shakespeare."

Emily stiffened. "I thought I dreamed that."

His charming grin took her breath away. "No, but you looked dreamy."

If her muscles weren't bunched before, they were now.

"Dylan put the microphone pack on the princess. They're on the move," Brad called out. "Position yourself."

"That's my cue to fade into the background." Emily moved toward the terrace where she would watch, but be out of the way.

Luc fiddled with his microphone pack. "Wish me luck."

She flashed an encouraging smile. "You don't need luck. She'll love you."

A flash of brilliant colors, almost like a painting or tapestry, appeared in the doorway.

Emily hurried onto the terrace.

Aldo, looking sharp in his butler's uniform, stood by the doorway. "Her Royal Highness Princess Marguerite Beatrix Annamarie of Mariposa."

Emily held her breath in anticipation. This could be Luc's future wife.

Marguerite stepped into the drawing room.

Huh? Emily did a double take. Leaned forward toward the drawing room window. Squinted.

Oh, no. Her breath rushed out as if someone had punched her in the gut. A butterfly. The woman was dressed as a butterfly complete with wings and antennae. Was the intricate design on the princess's face temporary or a permanent tattoo?

Princess Marguerite whispered something to the butler.

Aldo cleared his throat. "Also known as Princess Butterfly of Mariposa."

Luc glanced Emily's way, a surprising grin on his face and victory in his eyes.

Darn the man. She would have to concede defeat. But he must have had inside information. That was why he'd made the bet.

Princess Marguerite curtsied, spreading her skirt and translucent shimmery wings. The bouncing antennae matched her rainbow-colored hair.

Luc bowed. "Welcome, Your Highness. I hope you will enjoy tonight."

"And you, Your Highness."

He extended his arm, smiled. "Such an elaborate and colorful show of national pride."

Taking his hand, Marguerite beamed. "I do my best. My mother felt face paint might provide more options. She worried a tattoo might be too limiting in color schemes."

Not permanent. Thank goodness. Emily placed her hand over her pounding heart.

The princess looked up at Luc. "What do you think?"

His smile widened. "The queen of Mariposa is not only beautiful like her daughter, but intelligent too."

Marguerite's sigh could be heard outside.

Good job, Luc. Emily watched with a mix of fascination and a touch of regret. She shook off the latter emotion.

"I hear you're looking for a wife," Marguerite said. "My father is offering a large dowry to compensate for my well…"

"Lovely butterfly-ness," Luc offered.

Marguerite laughed. "Yes. The men aren't lining up outside the castle to ask for my hand."

"Their loss."

"Could be your gain…"

The words hung in the air. Emily wondered what Luc's answer would be and why she felt a sudden sense of dread.

AFTER MARGUERITE LEFT, Luc knocked on Emily's bedroom door. She'd disappeared during his date, and he'd decided dessert to celebrate his victory was in order and let her know he'd be collecting on his bet soon.

No answer, but he heard someone in the room.

He knocked again.

"Not right now." Emily's voice sounded raw.

"It's Luc."

"I-I…"

Something was going on. He opened the door.

The linen had been stripped from her bed. She was on the floor, clawing through the sheets. Her eyes gleamed. The always in-control, professional and practical ad exec looked as if she'd lost her best friend.

Luc placed the tray with éclairs on the closest table. "Emily?"

"I can't find her."

He kneeled by her side. "Who?"

"Miss Mousie." Emily sniffled. "I'd left her on the bed this morning, but when I came back tonight she was gone. I know she's just an old, dirty stuffed animal…"

"She's important to you. That's what matters." Her vulnerability tugged at Luc's heart. He pulled her against him, brushed his lips across her hair. "We'll find her. I've located tiny doll shoes and action figure lightsabers. A stuffed cat will be easier to find."

"I've gone through the sheets. Looked under the bed." She hiccupped. "Checked everywhere."

Luc caressed her face. A warm tear wet his fingertip. He

held her closer, felt the beat of her heart, wished he could make this better for her. "Did you check the laundry room?"

She straightened, looked up at him. "No. I thought she had to be in here."

"The housekeeper could have changed the linen and not seen her."

"That…" Emily blinked. "That makes total sense. I don't know why I didn't think of it."

She was too worried and upset to think logically, and Luc liked seeing this all-too-human side of her. He helped Emily to her feet. "Let's see if Miss M is there."

"Thanks, but I can do this myself."

"You could," he agreed. "But then I wouldn't get an éclair when you returned to your room. I know how much you like chocolate. There's no way you'll save one for me. They're that good. So I'm coming with you."

Gratitude filled Emily's gaze, made him feel important and stand taller.

Twenty minutes later, after searching through baskets of dirty and clean laundry, Luc found Miss Mousie in a tangle of freshly washed pillowcases and sheets.

He handed the stuffed animal to Emily. "Miss M looks a little whiter."

"Smells better, too." Emily held the stuffed cat to her heart. "Thanks."

Her smile brought unfamiliar peace. "Ready for an éclair?"

"Yes, but there's something I want first." She rose up on her tiptoes and kissed him.

The contact sent an explosion of sensation bursting through him. He wrapped both his arms around her. She went willingly against him. Moving her hips slightly and sending his temperature soaring.

Her lips moved over his. Familiar from the first kiss, but something felt different. Tongues danced, twisting and tangling.

She wove her fingers through his hair, arched against him.

A fire burned in his gut. "Emily…"

Forget the éclairs. He'd been searching for a princess, but Cinderella was right here in his arms. She might not be royal, but that didn't matter. Emily's sweet taste was the only thing that would satisfy him. She was all he wanted, all he needed tonight.

FIREWORKS DIDN'T BEGIN to describe the sensations pulsating through Emily with each of Luc's kisses. If Emily didn't stop kissing Luc, she wasn't going to be able to stop. Why had she kissed him?

Gratitude. That had been one reason. The others she didn't want to think about. His kisses were better than any dream.

Uh-oh, she was still kissing him. Emily drew back. Afraid

to meet Luc's gaze, she plumped a squished Miss Mousie. "I'm tired. I should get to bed. You're more than welcome to the éclairs."

"Look at me."

She did.

"Your kiss is tastier than any chocolate," he said.

Her heart melted. Her tongue felt too sizes too big. "Ditto."

That was the only word she didn't think she'd mangle.

The rich sound of his laughter made her want to invite him to her room, and not for dessert. At least not the one he'd brought.

Luc ran his fingertip along her jawline. "What am I going to do about you?"

Kiss her again. No, wrong answer. Emily couldn't let the situation get out of control or do something unprofessional. Though kissing the show's star in search of a wife wouldn't earn her an Employee of the Month Award.

"You don't need to do anything about me," she said. "I was thanking you for finding Miss Mousie. That's all."

Liar.

But she couldn't say she liked being with him. Talking, touching, kissing. Or how he'd made her feel not so alone and desperate tonight. Or a million other little things.

He grinned. "Perhaps you'll misplace her again."

Emily felt trapped in a box canyon, the only exit blocked by a stampeding herd of cattle. She needed to get away from

Luc before she said or did something she would regret. "I'll let you know if I do. Goodnight."

Self-preservation sent Emily bolting from the laundry room as if she was trying to outrun the cows. She thought Luc might have laughed before he said goodnight. But she wasn't about to glance back and see.

She couldn't. Even if a part of her wanted to. Badly.

THE NEXT MORNING, Emily sat in the villa's library, laptop open, tablet on, and cellphone at her ear. Her boss in San Diego had put her on hold, not caring that she was in Italy and he'd been the one to call after midnight San Diego time.

She'd been awake most of the night, thinking about Luc. Eating the two éclairs he'd left in her room had been almost as stupid as kissing him.

So what if he'd found her stuffed kitty? She wasn't a kid, even if she'd been acting like one. But spending her days with a real life prince who treated her like she was a Disney princess wasn't easy. Just this morning, she'd found herself humming One Day My Prince Will Come when she showered.

That was something Addie would have done before marrying Nick. Not Emily.

Luc had kissed several princesses at the end of their first dates. He liked to kiss women. She'd known that before meeting him. No reason to think their kisses meant anything other than two pairs of lips coming together.

She stared at the phone. Where was Don?

Luc peered in from the doorway. "Almost finished."

"Soon, I hope."

His hair swung over his face, making her wish she could push it back. She fought the urge to groan.

"Meet me at my special spot when you're finished," he said.

She had no idea what he wanted. Probably make plans for his second dates. "Be there as soon as I can."

Another minute passed. Silence filled the phone.

"I'm back." Don sounded not the least bit apologetic. Typical for her boss. "Every two-bit country and principality in Europe has a monarchy, yet Prince Luc has wasted a month of filming. Brad should be fired."

"Don't blame Brad or Prince Luc." Emily kept her voice calm. She'd worked for Don since she graduated from San Diego State University and was the one even Kevin Franks, the other founding partner, turned to during Don's tan-trums. "Kendra hired the show's so-called royalty consultant. Turns out she's one of your wife's sorority sisters who runs a gossip blog."

Don coughed. "I'll speak to my wife."

Lip service. He would say nothing. Kendra wore the pants in that relationship. Don was her yes-man with a titanium credit card that had no spending limit.

"We're finally making progress." Emily gave a quick

rundown, leaving out a few incidents, preferring to focus on those who'd agreed to second dates. "The final first date is today, then Luc begins the second dates. All the plans will be in place when I leave on Tuesday."

"Stay there."

She readjusted the phone at her ear. "What did you say?"

"Stay in Lake Como and see the filming through to the end."

"I have the energy drink presentation on Wednesday." Bringing in that account would bring millions to the firm and be the final tally mark she needed to be promoted to partner.

"Your presentation is excellent. Clint can handle it."

Clint Wallingford was Kendra's younger brother, an idiot who floated from account to account to keep his incompetence from causing too much damage.

"No." Emily didn't think she'd ever said that word to her boss, but she didn't care. Too much was riding on bringing in the new account. "I've spent months cultivating the relationship. I've worked non-stop on the presentation."

"You need to be a team player."

"I have been. But you told me last summer the only thing holding me back from being named a partner was bringing in a larger account. This is my chance."

"The show needs you."

Translation: Kendra needed her.

Too bad. Emily needed a promotion so she wouldn't

have to deal with being assigned to idiotic projects like this one. That gave her an idea. One that could backfire, but if Don agreed… "I'll stay and see the show to the end, if you promise I'll be named a partner when I return."

Silence greeted her on the opposite end of the phone.

She tapped her toes against the carpet, pressed her lips together to keep from saying a word.

"What if you don't find Prince Luc a fiancée?" Don asked.

"Then I don't deserve the promotion, but if he finds one…" Emily held her breath.

"Fine," Don said. "If the prince presents a fiancée at the palace, you'll be made a partner when you get back. If he doesn't, you won't see a promotion for at least two years. Deal?"

Air rushed from her lungs. She pumped her fist. She couldn't fail because of the foundation, but getting a promotion would be a dream come true. One she'd been working toward since she joined the firm seven years ago. "Yes, it's a deal."

Chapter Eight

L UC STOOD ON the lake's shore. Golden yellow, red and pink streaks colored the morning sky like a watercolor painting. Lake Como and this villa were as close to being magical places, as he'd found.

And Emily…

His heart danced a tango thinking about her. He hadn't known her long, but she was considerate, earnest and honest. She believed with enough hard work she wouldn't fail.

He believed she wouldn't, either.

If only he could find a princess exactly like her, especially one who kissed the way she did and made him want to be a better prince, a better man.

Footsteps sounded on the stairs behind him.

Luc didn't have to glance over his shoulder to know it was Emily. No one else would be coming down here this early.

"Such a pretty sky." Emily stood next to him. "What's

up?"

"I have a surprise."

She gave him a funny look. "Me, too."

"What's yours?" he asked, eager to hear hers.

"I'm not leaving tomorrow. I'll be around until the engagement presentation in Alvernia."

A mix of relief and warmth flowed through him. He hadn't wanted her to leave, but his reasons had been selfish, too selfish to ask her to stay. "Your choice or your boss's?"

"His."

"What about your meeting?"

"Someone else is going to handle it, but if the show is successful, I'll be promoted to partner."

Her wide grin told him this was good news. "Excellent."

"What's your surprise? Something you want to do on a second date because we need to make more plans?"

Forget about his upcoming dates. Emily wasn't leaving tomorrow. That was what mattered. "This was going to be a goodbye surprise, but now we'll have a happy-you're-staying celebration."

Luc led her to the spot he'd shown her a few days ago—a secluded beach surrounded by trees and a small lawn. Addie had decorated the area with tulle and flowers to resemble a fairy's hideaway.

Emily sucked in a breath. "Wow. This is so gorgeous."

The look of awe on her pretty face pleased him. He motioned to the fondue pot and assortment of fruits, cookies and cakes to dip. "There's chocolate and sparkling apple cider."

"You did this for me?" Her voice was soft.

He nodded. "It's never too early for dessert."

"Breakfast is highly overrated." She sat and picked up a fondue fork. "Especially when you have a lunch date in a couple hours."

"Who is this one with?"

Emily stuck a fork through a strawberry and dipped it into the chocolate. "Countess Maria-Therese Alexandra Louise of Christonia."

He'd rather not talk about other women, but now that she wasn't leaving, he didn't mind so much. "Her name sounds familiar."

"She said you've met though it was years ago. She's older than you. Thirty-one."

"I like older women." Especially twenty-eight-year-old blondes from San Diego.

"That's what I told her." Emily's smile faded. Concern replaced the warmth in her eyes. "There's something Maria-Therese wanted you to know. Off-camera."

"Sounds serious."

Emily nodded. "Maria-Therese dreamed of having a big family, but due to her emergency hysterectomy a year ago she can't have children. Fertility isn't one of your father's requirements, but she didn't know if it was one of yours."

Marriage hadn't been on his mind until his father

brought up the show. Luc had never thought about having children of his own. Perhaps if he loved the woman he married. He looked at Emily, felt a weird feeling in his stomach. Chocolate for breakfast might not have been the best idea.

"It's not a requirement." He poured himself a glass of sparkling cider. "I'm no longer included in the line of succession now that Bernard and Leo have children. Adoption is always an option too."

Emily's smile returned. "Good. The Countess will be pleased. She was worried."

"She admitted that to you?"

"She wanted to be completely open and honest. She's...gone through a hard time."

"Family issues?"

Emily nodded. "Maria-Therese was engaged to her country's crown prince. They fell in love as teenagers, but after her surgery, he canceled their engagement and married her younger sister in order to keep the line of succession going. The tension between sisters led to Maria-Therese being banished. She's a woman without a country, living in Italy with a great aunt, cut off from the rest of her family. I feel so bad for her."

The compassion and concern in Emily's voice wrapped around Luc's heart. He scooted closer to her until his thigh touched hers.

"How could you ever think you weren't nice?" he asked.

"I said I wasn't mean."

"At least not on purpose."

She stuck a square of pound cake into the fondue pot. "You couldn't remember my name that morning, yet you know what I said?"

"You intrigue me, Emily Rodgers."

"Well, you baffle the hell out of me, Prince Luc."

He laughed.

Before she could pull the piece out, he kissed her on the lips. She tasted like chocolate.

He wanted to deepen the kiss, but she backed away. "We shouldn't."

"What?"

"Kiss." Her voice cracked. "We need to focus, can't afford distractions. Not with your foundation and my promotion."

"I know what's at stake." The children he helped were on his mind constantly. So was Emily. "But you and I…"

"Are working together to find you a wife." She took a deep breath. "That's all we are. All we can be."

Luc didn't want to accept that. "What if I want more?"

"I'm sorry, but there isn't more to have."

LATER THAT DAY, Emily waited at the Como San Giovanni station for the Countess's train to arrive from Milan. She couldn't stop thinking about Luc. If she hadn't stopped kissing him, she wasn't sure what might have happened in that secluded, romantic fairy hideaway. She swallowed a sigh.

Tourists arrived and left in steady streams. Some wore backpacks. Others rolled their luggage. A hardy few carried hard-sided suitcases.

A bus pulled away from the station as another arrived. Taxis honked. Someone yelled.

So different from the villa. Though an underlying tension kept the place from being peaceful. The ticking clock of finding Luc a fiancée or Emily's attraction to him? Maybe a combination.

A text beeped. Must be the Countess. Emily glanced at her phone. Luc. The funny feeling in the pit of her stomach anytime she thought of him returned.

He had stayed at the villa. The camera crew, too. Nick had decided a busy train station was not the place for the prince to be seen, let alone filmed. She read his text.

Luc: *Is she hot?*

Hot? Of course he would want to know that.

Emily: *She's not here yet. But she looked elegant in her official state photograph.*
Luc: *Elegant doesn't = hot*

Emily groaned. Using her smart phone, she searched for a hot picture of the Countess. Didn't take long to find a beach shot. She wore a bikini bottom and held a hat in front her chest while standing on sand. Her long dark hair was wet and tousled.

Not elegant. Hot.

On a scale of 1 to 10, she was an 11.

Emily sighed, feeling dejected and… jealous.

That was odd. And disturbing.

But this wasn't about her. She should be happy he had another first date, not feel icky and uncertain and wishing she was a long-lost member of a royal family. She attached the picture and hit send.

> **Emily:** Is this hot enough for you?
>
> **Luc:** I suppose. But if you must know, I prefer blondes.

Emily ignored the urge to squee. That wasn't her style. But she couldn't allow Luc's remark to go without a reply.

> **Emily:** She might be willing to dye her hair, but don't ask until after the third date.
>
> **Luc:** Hahaha
>
> **Emily:** I know. I crack myself up sometimes.

A train arrived. A few minutes later, a woman with brunette hair in a French twist walked toward her. She wore a lime green designer suit. Something you might see on a Milan or Paris runway during Fashion Week. Her shoes, a pair of multi-colored strappy heels, had been in the latest edition of Vogue. A porter wheeled a cart of luggage behind her.

Elegant. Hot. Royal.

One thought ran through Emily's mind. Countess Maria-Therese of Christonia was perfect for Luc. Emily hadn't felt this way about any of the other princesses, but here, now, she could see Luc and the Countess together, as a couple, as husband and wife.

Emily's shoulders sagged. A hippo seemed to be standing on her chest. Each breath took effort. Hurt.

She had no idea what was going on or why she felt this way, but maybe her promotion wasn't the worst thing she could lose on this trip.

CAMERAS ROLLING, LUC stood in the music room and toyed with keys on the grand piano. Natural light filtered in through the windows. The Countess would be arriving soon.

His final first date. One of the women he'd met, perhaps the Countess herself, would be his bride. His breath caught, imagining his wedding day. He saw Emily at his side.

I'm sorry, but there isn't more to have.

She was correct.

His father would never approve of her.

But that didn't make Luc like her less or not want to kiss her again. He had to think of the foundation. That would put these crazy thoughts about the pretty American to rest, help him focus on the royals he could marry.

Feminine voices sounded on the staircase. One of them

he recognized; one he didn't.

Luc adjusted his tie, checked that his shirt was properly tucked in, breathed deeply.

Emily entered first. Her smile had to be a good sign. "This is Countess Maria-Therese Alexandra Louise of Christonia."

A tall, slender woman walked into the room. She was poised and beautiful. Her make up was perfectly applied. Not a hair out of place.

The Countess stopped in the center of the room and curtsied, a practiced move given the precision and her tight above the knee skirt. "Delighted to make your acquaintance again, Your Highness."

"The pleasure is mine, Countess."

He walked toward her. She smelled exotic, a mixture of jasmine, vanilla and maybe a hint of sandalwood. The woman was as elegant and hot, as Emily had said, a desirable combination for both a princess and a wife. But he had to force his gaze off Emily, who could hold her own against any woman.

"Please call me Luc."

She extended her arm. "I'm Maria-Therese."

Luc raised her hand to his mouth and kissed the top. Her smooth skin was a perfect ivory color, no scars or blemishes. He lowered her arm, then let go. "Welcome to Lake Como."

She glanced around. If she noticed the cameras pointed at her, she didn't let on. "A luxurious villa. Stunning design and decor."

"The grounds are my favorite part if you'd care for a tour."

Emily stood in a corner behind Dylan and his sound equipment. She bit her lip.

"I would love one," Maria-Therese said.

He motioned her to the French doors. "Let's start on the terrace."

She walked outside. Wes and Conrad followed with their cameras. Dylan and Brad were right behind. Emily stayed where she was.

"See you later," he mouthed to her.

She whispered, "Have fun."

"I will. You've done well with Maria-Therese."

Luc expected to see a big smile on Emily's face, but the corners of her mouth barely curved upright. Her face looked tight, her eyes sad. He wondered why.

TWO DAYS LATER, three princesses and one countess joined Luc at a local hospital. Going out on a group date seemed strange, but Emily explained this was the best way for him to get to know the four women better in the shortest amount of time. Brad agreed.

Who was Luc to argue? He could think of worse things than spending time with four beautiful women. Especially with Emily in the background making sure things ran smoothly. She carried bags full of toys and books to give to the children.

After visiting patient rooms, Luc could see that two of the princesses—Brigitte, who was the youngest, and Jemma, the astrophysicist—weren't as comfortable with the children as Maria-Therese and Sophie, the social worker. But that wasn't a deal breaker to Luc. Not everyone had experience with kids, including princesses.

Maria-Therese carried one of the bags of toys. "I love seeing the big smiles when the girls meet real-life princesses."

"Meeting a countess is just as special," Luc said.

Jemma glared. A smile appeared a second too late. She had a brilliant mind and was accomplished, but she might not be the best choice if her royal title made her feel superior.

That left three—Brigitte, Maria-Therese and Sophie.

"I want to mention a new treatment I read about to one of the doctors. It might help that little boy named Marko we visited." Sophie walked in the other direction from them. Luc was impressed how dedicated the princess from Alistonia was to helping others. She'd be an asset to the foundation, but was she the right woman for him? He needed more time to figure that out.

In a room with a little girl named Gia, who wore an oxygen tube, Luc sat on the edge of her bed while she told him about her stuffed animal named Socks.

"You see it's made out of a sock, sir." Gia raised the sock monkey in the air. "That seemed like the most perfect name."

"Socks is the absolute right name." Luc rubbed his chin. "Do you think Socks might like a new friend to play with?"

Gia's eyes widened.

A cellphone rang. Princess Brigitte removed her phone from her pocket and walked out of the room without saying a word.

Now that was a deal breaker. He'd mentally crossed Jemma off the list. Now it was Brigitte's turn. That left Sophie and Maria-Therese. Looked like Emily was right again. This group date was a good way for him to get to know the women better.

"Where were we?" Luc asked.

"A new friend." Maria-Therese reached into one of the bags and pulled out a purple stuffed animal. "Do you think Socks will want to be friends with an elephant?"

"Oh, yes." Gia took the elephant. "And we'll have to think of the best name. Thank you."

"You're welcome." Maria-Therese moved to the other side of Gia's bed. "Promise me you'll take good care of Socks and the elephant."

Gia hugged the two stuffed animals. "I will."

"And do what the doctors tell you," Maria-Therese continued.

Gia nodded.

"Good. I want to hear that you're feeling better." Maria-Therese touched the little girl's hand. The compassion in the countess's eyes reminded Luc of how Emily had acted with Vivianca and Gretchen.

Emily.

Maybe that was why he felt so comfortable with Maria-Therese. She was the most like Emily. Not in looks or personality or style, but in the way she cared for others. Was that enough to build a marriage upon?

Was Countess Maria-Therese his Cinderella? Or was Princess Sophie his future wife? At least he had a few more days to get to know them better until he had to propose.

They said goodbye to Gia, then walked out of the room.

Maria-Therese smiled at him. "What's on the schedule after we're finished here?"

He pictured the itinerary for the day. They would return to the villa where a surprise awaited them before lunch. "How do you feel about puppies?"

FOUR DAYS LATER, as the sun lowered toward the horizon, Emily sat on the boat dock. Her legs hung over the edge and her toes swung back and forth skimming the water.

She leaned back on her arms and lifted her face to the red sky. Her role here had been to find Luc a bride. She'd succeeded the way she knew she would. The hospital visit had been the deciding factor in sending two princesses—Brigitte and Jemma—home. Playing with the puppies that afternoon had reaffirmed his choice of the two—Maria-

Therese and Sophie—to stay.

But since the two royal women had arrived at the villa, everything had changed.

No more texts.

No more jokes.

No late night treats.

No more kisses.

Okay, Emily had told Luc they should stop kissing. She just thought he might try to steal one or two. Going cold turkey sucked.

She knew Luc had needed this time to decide between Maria-Therese and Sophie, even if Emily had known what his decision should be. And she'd been correct.

Maria-Therese was his choice. Last night, Sophie had left the villa in tears.

"Here you are." Luc walked toward Emily. His steps sounded on the dock, sending a bird flying. "I was wondering where you were hiding."

Emily glanced to her left. A wide smile reached all the way to his eyes. "Not hiding, relaxing."

"Never thought I'd see you relax."

"A new experience. One I'm enjoying." She peered around him. "Where's Maria-Therese?"

"Being filmed in one of the villages. Brad wanted some footage of her alone." He sat next to Emily. "So here I am. No cameras or microphones or royalty following me around. I feel like a bird released from a cage for the first time in days."

"You look like you've been enjoying yourself with two women vying for your attention." Emily cringed at the tone of her voice. She needed to retract the claws.

"How would you know? You haven't been around."

But she had. Not exactly spying or stalking. A better term might be lurking. "The villa isn't that big."

"A little over five acres of grounds and fifteen thousand square feet inside."

"Hard to miss with the crew following you." Or the sound of laughter wherever he and Maria-Therese went.

Not that Emily cared. That much anyway.

"I wanted to tell you—" he rubbed his lips together "—I asked Maria-Therese to marry me."

Emily's jaw dropped. She closed her mouth, but sat stunned, as if someone had just told her Clint Wallingford had gotten her promotion. But she thought Luc would have told her his plan, not just proposed without saying something to her first.

She moistened her dry lips. "Maria-Therese is perfect for you. Congratulations."

The fact Emily managed to say a five-syllable word without having her voice crack had to be a record.

"We haven't made an official announcement." His gaze didn't meet hers, and for that she was grateful. "We're working out some details first. Emily…"

She looked up at him. "What?"

He touched her shoulder. "Thank you for finding me a royal bride."

Emily swallowed. She should be happy, not feeling like someone stole Miss Mousie. "You're welcome."

"I hope you'll be in Alvernia for the engagement presentation."

She nodded, not trusting her voice. Her boss and his wife would be there also. She hoped Don offered the partnership in Alvernia instead of making her wait until they returned to San Diego. That might make her feel…better.

Now she was being silly.

This was what she'd been working toward since she arrived in Europe. The engagement presentation, a royal custom, would secure Luc's place in his family. He would keep his title, his land, and his money. Most importantly, his good work with the foundation would continue. And she would have her partnership. She should be happy. Thrilled.

She forced a smile, but the muscles around her mouth fought her. "Told you we'd be successful.

"I knew you wouldn't fail me." Luc sounded pleased. "Life as I know it will remain the same."

Hers would be changed forever.

Not because of her job. Work no longer seemed as important. But his Royal Highness Lucas Alexander Leopold Casimir von Rexburg had touched her heart with his kindness, his generosity, his sense of humor and his kisses.

A royal engagement ring sized lump burned in her

throat.

No. No. No.

She'd fallen for Luc. Probably the first day they'd met when she saw him with Vivianca. But Emily had been in denial; too scared to admit what she was feeling when her job was to find him a wife.

But she had and fallen hard.

No regrets.

Yeah, right.

She didn't know where to start with the regrets. She should have never kissed him, never told him about her parents or listened to him talk about his family, never allowed him into her heart.

But she had.

And she…

I love him.

Oh, no. She loved Luc.

He'd shown her how life could be so much more than work and for that she would be grateful. She no longer needed to define herself by what she did for a living and her ability to take care of herself. She could laugh, have fun, relax.

Like now.

Except she felt more tense and shivery, than relaxed.

He leaned toward her, his mouth inches from hers. The desire in his eyes matched hers for him. He wanted to kiss her. She wanted him to kiss her.

One last kiss.

What was she doing? Emily scooted away, nearly slipping off the dock. "We can't. You proposed to Maria-Therese."

"The proposal is not official until the engagement presentation."

Emily kept backing away from him. "Semantics. You don't need me now."

"I do need you."

The longing in his voice caused a physical ache inside her. "My job was to find you a bride. I did. Now you'll have a wife to help you."

And Emily would have…her promotion. She had the feeling Luc ended up with the better deal.

Chapter Nine

BEING BACK AT the palace made Luc feel like an imposter. He wasn't thinking about his fiancée. Emily was the only woman on his mind. He needed to do something about that.

The production crew moved equipment into the throne room for tomorrow's engagement presentation. He found Brad reviewing the ceremony's schedule with her. She looked lovely in a pair of pants with a frilly pale green shirt.

"Can I borrow Emily?" Luc asked.

"Go ahead, sir." Brad checked what Dylan was doing. "We've got cameras and lighting to work on."

Emily's tired eyes made Luc wonder if she'd been experiencing the same difficulty sleeping as him.

"Come." Luc motioned for her to follow. "I have something to show you."

She rose, wiping her hands against her thighs. The black fabric stretched across her hips and thighs, making him jealous of the pair of pants. She straightened the hem of her shirt.

"Where are we going?" she asked.

He placed his index finger by her lips, desperate to touch her. "Shhh. The palace is full of secrets."

Her smile brightened her face. "Lots of skeletons in closets."

"You have no idea." He led her into the music room where a grand piano resided in one corner and a harp in the other. "Close your eyes."

"Why?"

He fought the urge to kiss her to stop the questions. "Time to put away your analytical side and have fun."

"If you say so." She closed her eyes.

He pulled back a fake bookcase to open the hidden door behind. "Keep them closed."

"What's taking so long?"

"Patience." He held her hand. "Walk with me. But don't open your eyes until I tell you. I won't let you fall."

"Isn't that my line?"

"Not today." Inside the secret room, he reset the bookcase, then the door. "You may open your eyes."

She did. Blinked. "What is this place?"

"A secret hideaway. During the Great Wars, the royal family stored artwork and other valuables here. Now, this is where we go to escape."

Emily explored. "Who knows about this room?"

"Only the royal family. That's why you had to keep your eyes closed. Rules."

She ran her fingers across a leather sofa. "The ultimate man cave."

"I'm the only one who uses the room."

She looked around, then at him. "Thank you for bringing me here."

"You're the first."

"I'm honored."

He walked toward her with a sense of purpose. "I wanted you to see this place, but I brought you here for another reason. I never collected on our bet over Princess Marguerite. It's time to claim my winnings."

Emily wet her lips. "What do you want?"

"A goodbye kiss." He touched her lips with his finger. "Before you say no, I want you to know Maria-Therese is not here. She's at her great aunt's house packing her belongings and doesn't arrive till tomorrow. She knows there have been women in my life, ones I should say goodbye to."

"Is that what I am?"

He cupped her face. "I wish I knew what you were."

Emily turned so he wasn't touching her. "Well, the bet was for anything. I guess a kiss counts, and this place seems private enough. But no tongue action."

"I'm good with that."

She planted her lips against his with a hunger that surprised him and turned him on. This was his best bet ever.

And to whatever great-great-great-great relative had built this secret hideaway, Luc had one thing to say.

Thank you.

THE MORNING OF the engagement presentation, Emily sat across from her boss, Don, in the hotel's dining room. She sipped from her second cup of coffee, desperate for a jolt of caffeine to keep her going. She hadn't slept for more than an hour or two, working on Luc's engagement present and thinking about her time with him in the secret room.

One last kiss.

No regrets.

Only memories. Good ones. A few bittersweet ones too.

But she'd met her goal. Found the prince his Cinderella. In a few hours, Luc would slip his royal engagement ring on Maria-Therese's finger.

Emily glanced at her bare left hand. Ignored the way her insides twisted. She set her cup on the table. "I hope Kendra is pleased with the footage from Lake Como."

"She's sure she has another hit on her hands." Don raised his glass of orange juice. "You've succeeded where others have failed. Congrats."

Knowing Emily would be made a partner had kept her going. So what if she fell in love? No reason to cry over Luc. He was happy. She needed to focus on work. "Thank you. I'm excited to see what I can do as a partner."

"About that." Don stared into his juice glass. "You're going to have to wait until next year for your promotion."

She blinked as if that would change what she'd heard or enable her to see that he was teasing. Except Don's facial expression remained serious. He hadn't been kidding.

She stared in disbelief. "We had a deal."

"Yes, but a year isn't that long," Don said. "Kendra's idea for a royal wedding show might get picked up by a major network. Since you're familiar with the people involved—"

"You gave your word. I deserve to be made a partner now."

Don swirled his juice cup. "What you think you deserve doesn't align with our view of you at the agency."

"I don't understand."

"You're a worker bee, Emily. You get whatever task is assigned to you completed. You've done a lot for the agency, but I'll be honest. You don't show the necessary creativity and initiative to be named a partner. By next year—"

"Bull." Her temperature spiraled. "I've worked my butt off since I joined the company. My creativity and initiative is apparent on every single project, including your wife's TV shows."

"Kendra's royal wedding series will give you more visibility."

"I have plenty of that at the agency. I don't want to work on any more TV shows."

"You don't have a choice."

Realization dawned. "I would if I was a partner."

Don choked on his juice. "I have no idea what you're talking about."

Emily not being named a partner had nothing to do with her abilities, but everything to do with Kendra Peabody. "Your wife doesn't want you to promote me."

"Kendra has no say at the ad agency."

"Then make me a partner."

"I can't do that. Continue to work hard—"

"Not good enough."

"That's all I can offer."

Emily thought about how hard she'd worked these past seven years, sacrificing her personal life and giving up relationships that interfered with her job. All she'd wanted was the promotion. She still wanted to be a partner. But she wouldn't put in another year working crazy hours and reality TV projects for a temper-tantrum throwing, selfish boss.

Because of Luc, she knew there was more to life than work. For all she knew, Don would drag this out another seven years. She'd be no different than her mother, waiting for her dad to change his mind and decide he wanted them. No way. "I quit."

Don's mouth gaped. "You can't quit."

"I just did." A thousand pound weight lifted off Emily's shoulders. "I'll work through the engagement presentation, then I'm finished."

"You're required to give notice."

"I'm giving you notice. I'll email HR when I get back to my room." She should be shocked, upset, but the only thing she felt was contentment. A new feeling for her. "I've never taken a day of vacation or sick time in the seven years I've been at the agency. I'm sure I have more than enough paid time off to cover my two weeks notice."

"Now, wait a minute." Don leaned over the table. A smarmy smile formed. "Perhaps I was hasty in saying a year. Maybe in six months…"

"No, thanks." She felt almost giddy. "I'm sure there's another ad agency who'll love to find a worker bee like me."

"I won't give you a recommendation."

His words didn't surprise her. One more reason she needed to get away from Peabody-Franks. "Your choice, but I have copies of my reviews as well as the letters that accompanied my bonuses. Perhaps Kevin will give me one."

Emily rose. And though the unknown was scary for someone who planned everything out the way she did, she knew in her heart she'd made the right choice about her job.

If only she had a choice with Luc.

THAT AFTERNOON, LUC stood in the foyer outside the palace's throne room. He peeked through the cracked doors. His parents sat in their impressive throne chairs, wearing the royal crown and tiara and fur-lined capes draped over their shoulders. His father held a scepter, rumored to have been stolen in the thirteenth century from an evil Germanic despot. The story changed with each king's coronation.

Maria-Therese stood at Luc's side. "Are you ready?"

Nodding, Luc resisted the urge to tug at his collar. Too many eyes were watching, waiting for him to make a mistake, and embarrass his family. He wouldn't. Emily was correct. The only expectations he needed to live up to were his own. He wished he could see her.

Duty first.

Luc straightened. "I've been preparing for this since my eldest brother became engaged."

Six siblings had participated in the ceremony before Luc. He would be the last unless his brother, Leo, a widower with two young children, repeated the ceremony if he remarried. In the royal family, divorce wasn't an option if a couple wanted to separate, only death. An archaic custom, that meant bad marriages were to be endured for the sake of Alvernia and the monarchy.

"We had more fun playing tag and hide-and-seek in here when we were younger, than practicing."

"Your parents allowed that?" Maria-Therese sounded shocked. Luc didn't blame her.

"No, the throne room was off-limits, but that didn't stop us from sneaking in on a rainy day."

"Almost time, sir." Nick used the formal address protocol demanded at the palace.

Luc nodded an acknowledgment. He glanced into the

room once again.

Tapestries, depicting scenes from Alvernia's past, covered the walls made of stone. He hoped Emily had seen the panels before the lights and cameras were set up yesterday.

Three elaborate chandeliers hung from the ceiling, each a testament to a beloved ruler. Antlers for King Gregor the Hunter. Swords for King Phillip the Fighter. Arrows for King Alexander the Brave.

So much history and accomplishment.

A sense of pride filled Luc. Each man had left a legacy, and Luc, though he would never rule, wanted to leave one, too. Emily believed he would with Dream Big Alvernia. He hoped she was right. Too bad she couldn't be the one to help him take the foundation to the next level.

Luc glanced over at Maria-Therese. She wore a stylish yellow dress with a blue and red sash, the colors of her former country. "You look lovely."

Her smile widened. "Emily took me shopping. She helped me pick out this dress and the shoes."

Was there anything his Emily couldn't do? "It's perfect."

"Thank you." Maria-Therese touched one of the medals on his uniform. "I didn't realize you were in the military."

"All royal family members, regardless of gender, serve. Length of active duty varies. Being the youngest, mine was brief due to a request from the Queen."

"You're still her baby."

"I hope that will change once I'm married."

Maria-Therese looked around. "If this is what your family does for an engagement, I'm intimidated to imagine what our wedding will be like."

Her smile reached her eyes, letting him know she was joking.

He smiled back. "My family goes overboard with ceremonial events, but especially weddings."

"Make it easy on yourselves and elope," Nick suggested.

"We can't," Luc and Maria-Therese said at the same time. And then laughed.

He waited to feel a connection or spark. Nothing. If this had been Emily...

Coronets sounded. A crier read from a scroll, announcing their names and presenting them to the king and queen.

"That's our cue," Luc said.

Maria-Therese nodded once, straightened her shoulders and smiled. So did he, the way he'd been trained by Mrs. Renault.

He extended his left arm. Maria-Therese laid her right forearm and hand on top of his. The two stepped with their right feet at the same time.

This was it. Luc's moment to shine with the woman he was going to marry. But one thought hammered through his brain. The wrong woman was being presented to his parents.

Emily should be on his arm.

He...loved her.

He wanted to marry her.

Only her.

What in the hell was he doing with Maria-Therese?

THE PALACE BUZZED with excitement. Emily, too. Kevin Franks, Don's original partner, had called and asked her to reconsider leaving the ad agency, but she wasn't going back.

Time to move on.

But to what?

The question both scared and exhilarated her. She wanted more balance in her life. She wanted love. Luc.

Her heart twisted as if someone was trying to squeeze the blood from it.

Well, maybe someone like him…

She took a chocolate-drenched crème puff from the dessert table, then headed onto the balcony.

"Hiding?" Luc asked.

Her heart lodged in her throat. She'd only seen him at a distance during the presentation, but he looked handsomer up close in his uniform and sash. She fought the urge to move toward him.

She raised her dessert plate. "I didn't want anyone to see I'm having another crème puff."

"Your second?"

She wiped her mouth with a napkin. "Third."

His smile was a combination of sexy and sweet, like his kiss. "Addicted to Alvernia's pastries."

"Among other things." She forced her gaze away from his lips.

He walked toward her. Each step sounded a gong in her head. "Such as?"

"The landscape and gorgeous views of the Alps."

"Anything else?"

"The people." She needed to speak in general terms. "So friendly and welcoming."

Luc stood next to her. His heat and scent and strength made her want to feel his arms around her one more time. "Any specific people?"

"Perhaps."

He brushed a strand of hair behind her ear. "Perhaps me?"

The hope in his voice sent her pulse skittering every which way, like a bowl of M&Ms dropped on a hardwood floor. She couldn't answer him. Not here.

Emily tightened her grip on the plate. She felt uncertain.

"Luc..." She wasn't using proper protocol, but remembering to say the correct words wasn't easy when she'd rather call him *my love*. "Watching you during the ceremony brought a lump to my throat, sir."

"You didn't answer my question."

"I...I can't." Because if Emily did, she'd give herself—her heart—away. But she could tell him something else. "I quit my job."

His eyes widened with a look of shock. His lips parted.

He started to speak, then stopped himself. He laced his fingers with hers. "I don't understand. You love your job."

"I thought I did, but I realized that's not what I want any longer. So far no buyer's remorse. I'll see how I feel tomorrow, but right now I want to twirl and shout."

"That doesn't sound like you."

"I know. And that's a good thing, I think."

"It is." He raised their linked hands and spun her in a pirouette. "What are you going to do?"

"For the first time in my life, I haven't got a clue. And that's okay too."

He stared into her eyes. "I have a suggestion."

"What?"

"Stay in Alvernia."

As if that were a possibility. She half-laughed. "Yeah, right."

"I'm serious," he said. "You're all I thought about during the presentation."

A thrill ran through her. She wanted to kiss him, but reality shouted at her with a blow horn. "Your parents looked pleased."

"They adore Maria-Therese." He reached up and ran a fingertip along Emily's jawline. "I adore you."

She nearly collapsed against him with need. But she knew better. Needing her father had nearly killed her mother. Emily might want Luc, but she didn't need him. Or anyone.

She leaned away from him. "Please don't. You have Maria-Therese."

"I want you."

Air rushed from her lungs. She was afraid to hope.

A thoughtful expression crossed his face. "Forget San Diego. Work at the foundation, broaden our donation pool with your advertising expertise, take Dream Big Alvernia to the next level."

She stiffened. "You're offering me a job?"

"You understand what the foundation means to me. We would not only work together, but we could be together."

"What about Maria-Therese?"

"We aren't in love. I respect her and look forward to deepening our friendship over the course of our marriage."

Emily was confused. "If you're marrying her, how will we be together?"

"I own a large estate with many houses. You could live in one of them. You and I can have a family. You'd be a wonderful mother."

"Wait a minute." She shook her head, as if trying to get water out of her ears. "You want to have a family with me when you're married to another woman?"

"Married in name only. Maria-Therese is still getting over her brother-in-law."

"That doesn't change the fact I'd be your mistress. The other woman."

"Semantics." He brushed his hand through the air as if

sweeping away Emily's concerns like a gnat. "I'm asking you to be part of my life. Forever."

"A life we can't share beyond the two of us. A life full of secrets and hurt."

"No one will get hurt."

Emily couldn't believe this was happening. That he was asking her to do this. She took a breath. And another. "I can't—won't—be involved with a married man. Not after what my dad put my mom through with his cheating. His actions destroyed her and me. I thought you understood—"

"I do, but this is different."

"How so?"

"I care about you. I want you to be a part of my life. And this is the way to make that happen."

She laughed. It was either that or cry. "You are a true Alvernian with an unquenchable taste for pastries. You want your cake and to eat it too."

All the heartache of her childhood rushed to the surface, memories and pain she thought she'd buried. Watching her mother drink herself to oblivion. Knowing her father would rather be with his other children than her. Realizing she was the only one she could rely on, no one else.

Luc had just reaffirmed that last one.

"You can't have me." Her voice sounded hard, like her heart felt. "Not the way you want."

His face fell. She ignored the urge to comfort him. That wasn't her responsibility.

"I've been part of a forgotten family." She loved Luc, but she couldn't do this. "I can't be part of a secret one. I deserve better."

"There is no other way for us to be together." His jaw thrust forward. "We'll make this work. I'm not saying goodbye."

"You don't have to, but I do." Her throat tightened with loss, from the past and from now. "Goodbye, sir."

GOODBYE, SIR. LUC stood on the balcony alone. Emily's final words echoed in his head and ricocheted in his heart.

She was gone. He'd wanted to show her how much she meant to him. He thought she'd be happy he'd found a way for them to be together, not disgusted and offended that he wanted to be with her while married to someone else. Someone she'd found for him. A woman she knew he didn't love. A woman still getting over a past love.

"There you are." His mother joined him on the balcony. "Maria-Therese is looking for you."

"Give me a minute."

His mother came closer. Touched his cheek. "I know that look. What happened?"

"I…" He stared at the ground.

"Let me guess. This has to do with that American. The blonde from the TV show. The one you can't stop staring at."

"Her name is Emily."

"You're attracted to her."

"I asked her to stay in Alvernia. To be with me."

His mother tilted her head, as if in thought. "What about Maria-Therese?"

"Our marriage is one of necessity, not love."

"What did Emily say?"

"Goodbye. Her father cheated on her mother. She wants no part of being the other woman even though the situations are completely different."

"Oh, my son." His mother sighed. "The situations are exactly the same."

"I don't love Maria-Therese. She doesn't love me."

"Love is only one part of a marriage and cycles like the phases of the moon, especially after you have children. Being committed during the good and bad times is what makes a marriage successful, dare I say more so than love. There are days when I barely like your father, let alone love him. But I made a choice, and continue to make the choice, to love him and remain at his side. Not find a lover and live a secret fantasy instead."

Damn. He brushed his hand through his hair. "I screwed up."

She squeezed his shoulder. "Yes, you did. Apologize to Emily, then let her go."

"I don't know if I can do that."

His words brought another pause from his mother.

"Then you have a decision to make. What means the most? Your title and money? Or Emily?"

She did. Luc knew that in his heart. But he had his foundation to consider, all the children and their families, and he'd also proposed to Maria-Therese. She'd relocated to Alvernia and was planning to marry him.

Luc rubbed his forehead. What was he going to do?

Chapter Ten

T HE DAYS DRAGGED one into the next. Luc went through the motions of "planning" an impromptu engagement party. Thankfully his mother and Maria-Therese only wanted him to nod every once in a while.

Luc still had no idea what to do about Emily. He appreciated Maria-Therese and what she was doing for him. She'd embraced her role as his fiancée. He wanted to do the same for her. But his every thought, his every breath, his every heartbeat was about Emily.

He had no idea where she was. Still in Alvernia or back in San Diego? Somewhere else?

At his engagement party, the sounds of laughter and the chime of crystal champagne flutes toasting became too much for Luc. He sought refuge on the balcony, the same place where Emily had said goodbye.

Goodbye, not goodnight.

Air whooshed from his lungs. Memories threatened to

overwhelm him.

Goodnight, goodnight! Parting is such sweet sorrow, That I shall say goodnight till it be morrow.

If only he could go back to Lake Como… No, to the day they'd met at the hotel. He would do everything differently.

"Smile." Brad walked out onto the balcony. Conrad and Wes followed, cameras in hand. "It's almost over. Tonight will be the last footage we shoot. Unless you sign on for a sequel, and we're back to do the royal wedding."

Luc's stomach turned, but he kept a smile glued on his face. A wedding date hadn't been set. His mother had told him a minimum six-month engagement would be required for the royal wedding planning. He didn't mind waiting. Neither did Maria-Therese. She'd moved into a guesthouse here at the palace and seemed content.

"Nothing personal," Luc said. "But I hope this is the last time I see you and your cameras."

Brad laughed. "Don't blame you, dude."

Dude. Luc preferred that to being called sir.

"Question time." Brad positioned his film crew. "How do you feel now that your search for Cinderella has come to an end?"

"I'm thrilled the glass slipper fit Maria-Therese. She will be a fine princess for Alvernia." Each word came without effort because what he said was true. "We have many things in common, and she's a huge fan of pastries."

Though not crème puffs like Emily. He hadn't offered

éclairs yet.

"So it's a match made in heaven?" Brad asked.

"If you want to call Lake Como heaven, then yes," Luc replied, being cautious with his word choice. "I shall carry fond memories of my time at the villa."

Especially the time spent with Emily—working, relaxing, kissing.

"If you could change one thing about your search for Cinderella, what would it be?" Brad asked.

That Emily was still part of his life. She wouldn't accept what he offered her, but he wasn't in a position to give her what she needed. Not if he wanted to satisfy his father, family, and Maria-Therese.

Brad repeated the question.

"I'm sorry it's taking me so long to answer," Luc said finally. "Finding a bride was harder than I thought it would be. There were missteps, a few mistakes, but thankfully I found my future wife. I would change...nothing."

Liar.

He would change everything, including the woman he chose to marry. But no one wanted to hear that. Not even himself.

"There you are." Maria-Therese sashayed to his side and kissed his cheek. Her elegant gown shimmered under the lights like a million and one tiny silver stars. "Your parents want us in the ballroom."

Her exotic perfume was a perfect match to her attire.

The smell was pleasant and expensive. But he missed the floral scent of Emily's shampoo.

"Let's go." His hand found the small of Maria-Therese's back. He waited for awareness to seep through him the way it had at Vivianca's cottage with Emily.

But nothing happened. No spark or hint of physical chemistry. Only respect and gratitude and friendship. That would be enough, wouldn't it?

The camera crew followed. Dylan met them on the way into the ballroom.

Luc escorted Maria-Therese to the front of the orchestra where the king and queen stood.

"Do you know what's going on?" Maria-Therese whispered.

He shook his head once, keeping a smile on his face. "I was hoping you might."

"This isn't something I planned. Maybe your mother did." Maria-Therese sounded worried.

He squeezed her hand. "I'm sure it's some formality or custom I don't remember."

They climbed the steps to join his parents on the dais.

His father smiled proudly. "I want to thank you for attending our youngest son's engagement party. Queen Lisbeth and I are thrilled with his choice. Welcome to the family, Maria-Therese."

She curtsied.

"We've recently discovered an activity of Luc's that he's

been keeping secret from us," his father continued.

The crowd tittered at the hint of scandal.

Luc stiffened. Given the two weeks he'd spent with Emily, he fought a rising panic. He didn't want to hurt her more or cause any pain to Maria-Therese.

She patted his upper arm.

He appreciated the support.

His father raised his hands to quiet the crowd. "Viral photos, scantily clad women, and champagne are not involved, but my son's Dream Big Alvernia foundation is."

What the…

"I'd like to share engagement wishes from a few special Alvernians," his father continued.

The lights dimmed. A screen lowered.

Luc had no idea what was going on, but he didn't like the attention his father was focusing on the foundation.

The words DREAM BIG ALVERNIA appeared, followed by a princess, Addie wearing a pink costume and a sparkling tiara. Smiling, she kneeled next to a familiar looking hospital bed. "What would you like to say to Prince Luc and Countess Maria-Therese?"

The camera zoomed in on Vivianca with a big smile on her face. She wore the tiara Luc had given her. "I want to say I love you, and I hope you live happily ever after."

The audience sighed.

A video from of one of his visits played. He was telling Vivianca a story about a beautiful princess while she painted his fingernails. Gretchen must have filmed that on her cellphone.

An interview with Gretchen came next. She spoke about the many nights Luc spent at the hospital never leaving Vivianca's side. About living on the third floor of an apartment building without an elevator and how Luc had moved them into the one level cottage. About how grateful she and Vivianca were to Dream Big Alvernia and Prince Luc.

"I'm so happy you found your princess." Vivianca beamed and waved a toy wand. "You deserve so much happiness for all you do and give."

A video with a second child he'd helped played. And another. And another. They followed a similar format, but each one touched Luc's heart. He might not share the same blood or name with these children, but each one was family—his family. He wiped his eyes.

The final shot showed his staff outside their office at his estate. Each one held balloons and signs. They shouted congratulations and welcomed Maria-Therese to the team.

Emily.

She'd done this. No one else knew about the children and his staff. No one else had use of a film crew and Addie.

But Emily had promised him...

"I had no idea you did all this for children and their families." Maria-Therese leaned close and whispered into his ear. "Perhaps you are Prince Charming."

Luc realized why Emily had done this.

Imagine how happy my future wife will be when she finds out about it.

She'd done this for him and Maria-Therese. That made his empty heart hurt more. "I'm just a man trying to do a little good."

"By giving yourself to those children and their families. Loving and helping them." Maria-Therese kissed his cheek. "You're amazing."

The clips continued. So much care and time must have gone into making the video. He couldn't imagine when Emily would have had time to—

After they'd returned from the villa.

After she'd said goodbye.

After he'd lost her respect.

After he'd lost her heart and her love forever.

Oh, Emily…

The video ended. The audience clapped.

His father quieted them. "This video was delivered to the palace. A private gift to Luc and Maria-Therese, but I wanted to share what Dream Big Alvernia does with everyone here tonight."

Luc understood how his father had ended up with the video. As a precaution for the royal family's safety, every package was opened by security.

"I couldn't be more surprised, impressed and proud of Luc. What he's done for these children and their families, and what he will continue to do with Maria-Therese by his side, needs to continue. Queen Lisbeth and I are donating ten million dollars to the Dream Big Alvernia Foundation as an engagement present to my son and his lovely bride."

Luc's mouth gaped. Marie-Therese gasped.

"I hope you agree this important work needs to continue and will support their Dream Big Alvernia foundation."

All eyes were upon him. The cameras filmed.

Luc searched for the right words to say. He settled for the basic of sentiments, all he could manage at the moment.

"For all the children served by Dream Big Alvernia, I thank you for your generosity, Your Majesties, from the bottom of my heart."

The next hour, Luc was besieged with questions and donations. He'd left Maria-Therese in the capable hands of his brother, Leo, and his two children, then went to find Brad.

"You made the video," Luc said to the producer.

Brad beamed. "Came out nicely, but I can't take the credit for Emily's hard work. She was the brain and the driving force, as usual. She made us promise no one would know about the video except you and Maria-Therese. That's my fault. I didn't know how deliveries at the palace worked."

"I understand, and I'm grateful."

"Emily deserves the thanks. She gathered the videos from families and sent Addie for interviews after your engagement presentation. She just finished yesterday. And now..." Brad shook his head. "We're going to miss her. She's one of a kind."

One of a kind.

Luc's kind.

Emily was the one he thought about before closing his eyes and when he woke up. Her kiss was how he wanted to start his day each morning and end each night.

He returned to the ballroom. Maria-Therese was dancing with Leo while his two children ran around them in a circle.

She would be the perfect princess, an asset to Alvernia, but he loved Emily. He couldn't deny the truth any longer.

He needed to talk to his fiancée and tell her how he felt. His love for Emily might not make a difference to Maria-Therese, and if not, he'd stand by his proposal to her. But if it did…

His heart pounded so loudly he was certain the entire ballroom could hear.

Perhaps this story could have a happy ending after all.

THE NEXT MORNING in her hotel, Emily packed her suitcase, showered and dressed. She wore jeans and a T-shirt, the only non-work clothes besides pajamas she'd brought to Alvernia.

Not one tear fell. And hadn't for eight hours. Progress.

Finally.

No more hiding away from reality. No more pity-parties. She needed to make the long journey home to San Diego.

And get her act together.

She checked her room one last time to make sure she

hadn't forgotten anything. Satisfied everything was packed, she left a tip for the housekeeping staff, put her purse over her shoulder, and then wheeled her luggage out of the room.

Her heart might be broken, but that didn't mean she couldn't function. Okay, the past few days had been impossibly hard. Somehow she'd managed to finish the engagement video, and thanks to Addie and Nick, Emily hadn't been alone. They'd provided food, an unending supply of chocolate, and shoulders to cry on. She thought about stopping by their room to say goodbye, but she didn't want to wake them.

Emily rode the elevator to the first floor. The doors opened, and she stepped into the lobby.

People milled about. Chatting, laughing, living. Classical music played, but a sad ballad about broken hearts and new beginnings would better match her mood.

Hard to believe only two weeks ago, she'd arrived with Addie. So much had changed since then.

Everything really.

She was unemployed and broken hearted now. Two things she never would have imagined herself being.

Focus.

She walked to the front desk and checked out of her room using her personal credit card. Her corporate one no longer worked. At least the agency hadn't canceled her airline ticket, but she'd received an email from Human Resources saying to pick up her personal belongings and return her ID badge, parking pass, and laptop.

The woman handed back Emily's credit card. "We hope you enjoyed your stay."

"Your hotel is lovely." She didn't know what else to say when a part of her wished she'd never heard of Alvernia or…him.

Luc.

Her eyes stung. She stared up at the frescoes on the ceiling and blinked the tears away. She'd cried enough.

She straightened. "Where do I wait for the taxi I hired to take me to the airport?"

"Take a seat. When your driver arrives, the bellhop will call your name."

"Thank you."

As Emily stepped away from the front desk, she heard her name being called.

Addie ran from the elevator and hugged her. "I was hoping you hadn't left. You didn't answer my texts."

"I muted my phone last night and must have forgotten to turn the sound back on."

"Did you sleep?"

"A little." This morning had been the first she hadn't watched the sunrise.

Addie's gaze narrowed. "You look better."

"I feel better." Not a lie. Emily didn't feel as hopeless this morning. She didn't have an action plan, but the thought of making one no longer paralyzed her. More progress.

"Don't go home. Come to Paris with us."

She loved Addie and Nick, but Emily needed a break from seeing two people so much in love. For the first time, she knew what she was missing out on by being alone. She wanted to find love once her bruised and aching heart healed.

Someday it would. At least she hoped so.

"Thanks," she said. "But I need to go home, turn in the things that don't belong to me and pick up my personal belongings."

"Don't even think about writing a resume and applying for jobs. You need a break. A vacation."

Emily nodded. That much she'd figured out in between sob-fests. "I'm going to take a staycation. I can't remember the last time I played tourist in San Diego and doing that fits my new budget."

"You'll have fun."

She was thinking her stay-at-home vacation would be more of a distraction than fun. "Thanks for coming to Alvernia. I don't know what I would have done if you hadn't been here."

"Thank you." Addie grinned, then counted off on her fingers. "I got to travel to Europe, see my husband, stay in a fabulous villa, dress up like a princess and visit with cute kids. This has been the second best trip of a lifetime."

"Your honeymoon in Fiji was number one."

"Thanks to you. I'm sorry things with Luc didn't work

out."

"I'll put him behind me and be standing tall soon enough. Just need to wash my big girl panties and put them back on."

Addie smiled. "That sounds more like the Emily I know."

Good. The wussy, sad, heartbroken person she'd become wasn't someone she liked being. "I'll text you when I get home."

"Ms. Rodgers," the bellhop called.

"Time to go." She hugged her friend. "Have a fabulous time in Paris. Send me a postcard."

"Enjoy your staycation."

Emily followed the bellhop outside. No cars were parked in front of the hotel. "I thought my ride was here."

The bellhop pointed down the street. "It's coming."

She saw a carriage being drawn by four white horses. "I didn't order that."

"I'll double-check." The bellhop ran inside.

The carriage resembled a pumpkin coach, only white not orange and with royal blue cushions. The uniformed driver wore an old-fashioned white wig complete with a ponytail.

Romantic.

Like Cinderella.

A vise tightened around her chest, squeezing her heart like a fist. She struggled to breathe.

Oh, no. Don't lose it.

The carriage stopped in front of her. A bride must be riding this to her wedding.

The thought cut Emily like a knife. She'd never been into fairy tales or one true love or happy endings. Damn Luc for making her want those things.

And more.

With him.

But this wasn't entirely his fault. She accepted her part. She'd been sent to find him a princess bride, not fall in love with the intended groom. He'd put his foundation and his family first. She understood that he had a duty, responsibilities. But she was angry at herself for not being more careful. She was the only one to blame for losing her heart to the prince.

"I made a mistake."

Luc?

That sounded like his voice. She glanced around, but didn't see him. Maybe her lack of sleep had caught up with her.

He walked around the front of the white horses. He wore red pants with a gold stripe down the sides of each leg, a white uniform jacket with gold braids on the shoulders and a blue sash worn diagonally across his chest. Ribbons with medals were pinned over his heart. He carried a glass slipper.

A real life Prince Charming.

She forced herself to breathe. "What are you doing here?"

"I came to apologize."

"Apology accepted." Nothing he said would change things between them. "I have a plane to catch."

"Try on the glass slipper."

"You already found your Cinderella."

"I did. You. Just took me a little while to realize it."

His words shattered what fragile grasp of control she had.

"Please. Don't." Her voice sounded raw like the hurt she felt. "Leave me alone."

"I can't. I don't want to lose you."

"You lost me. A glass shoe isn't going to make a difference. I won't be your mistress."

"Then be my wife." He came closer. "I love you."

Her mouth gaped. Blood roared through her veins.

No. This wasn't possible. "Maria-Therese—"

"Understands. Turns out she has much in common with my brother, Leo. He's a widower with two children. My father approves."

"Where does that leave you?"

He half-laughed. "I pray with you."

"You need to marry royalty."

"I have relinquished my title." He motioned to his costume. "Prince Charming is the only prince I will ever be."

The gesture touched her heart. But he was also being romantically stupid. "What if I don't want to be with you? You've given up your title for nothing."

"Not for nothing." Sunlight sent prisms reflecting off the glass shoe. "If you say no, I'll whisk you away to a quiet, secluded place so we can go through that fall-in-love questionnaire you mentioned the first day we met."

She couldn't give in. Not even if her heart wanted her to surrender. Self-preservation was telling her to run. Fast. "We won't get far in a carriage."

"No, but we'd be traveling in style."

"What about Dream Big Alvernia?"

"That's under negotiation. Being the family's scapegoat means I know where all the recent skeletons are buried. Not that I'd betray family secrets, but the King doesn't know that. His ten million dollar engagement present would go a long way as far as hush money."

"Hush money to his own son?"

"Relinquishing my title meant being disowned, though my mother isn't going to let that happen without a fight, and the video you've made has insured country-wide support of the foundation." Holding her hand, Luc kneeled on the sidewalk. "I've said the words once, but I'll say them a million times more. I love you, Emily Rodgers. I love how driven you are. I love how hard you work. I love how you want only the best for others. I love how you kiss. I want to be with you, only you. Will you marry me?"

Logic told her to scream no. Neither had jobs. Luc would end up hating her for giving up his title.

But her heart countered each argument with a reminder of the good times they'd had together, his kind heart and his generosity to the children of Alvernia. Not to mention his hot kisses.

He loved her, and the feeling was mutual.

They might not have a storybook love complete with castles and tiaras, but they would have each other. That was enough.

She smiled at him. "Let's see if the shoe fits…"

He removed her sandal and placed the glass slipper onto her foot. "A perfect fit."

"You've found your Cinderella."

Hope filled his eyes. "Does that mean…?"

"Yes." Joy flowed through her. "I would love to marry you."

He removed something from his pocket, then slid an emerald engagement ring onto her ring finger. "This ring was given to me by my grandmother, Queen Monique. She would have loved you."

He stood and kissed Emily, a kiss full of kindness and compassion and love. Her heart sighed, then burst into song. This man was all she wanted. Together they could make a difference in the lives of the children in Alvernia. Maybe in America too.

She pulled back, looked around, realized they were standing in full view of whoever was on the street. "Oh, no. Your proposal is going to be all over the Internet."

"Yes, but how I want it to be seen. Not shot by strangers and paparazzi. I had Nick run a diversion with the help of Leo and Maria-Therese." Luc motioned across the street where Brad and the crew stood with their gear. The four men waved. "I asked them to film my proposal. Our kids might want to see it someday."

Our kids. Emily liked the sound of that, especially if they resembled Luc. But their other kids—the ones they helped through the foundation—might want to see this and attend the wedding.

"A good thing you wore pants, not tights. Otherwise you would have totally embarrassed the kids."

"It's not too late," he said in a playful tone. "I could change."

"Forget the tights." She stared up at him with love. "I'd rather you kiss me again."

"My pleasure." He grinned. "Would you like a happily ever after with that kiss?"

"Of course, and with the kiss after that and the kiss after that one."

He laughed. "You can have whatever you like."

"Well, I've got you." Smiling, she raised her foot to show off the glass slipper. "But since you're offering, could I please have the other shoe?"

The End

If you enjoyed **The Cinderella Princess**, you will love the rest of the Royal Holiday series!

The Cinderella Princess by Melissa McClone

Her Secret Prince by Madeline Ash

His Defiant Princess by Kathleen O'Brien

His Forbidden Princess by Jeannie Moon

Available at your favorite online retailer!

Enjoy more stories by Melissa McClone!

The Bar V5 Ranch Series

Home for Christmas

Mistletoe Magic

Kiss Me, Cowboy

Mistletoe Wedding

A Christmas Homecoming

Stand Alone Title

The Honeymoon Prize

Available at your favorite online retailer!

About the Author

Melissa McClone has published over twenty-five novels with Harlequin and been nominated for Romance Writers of America's RITA award. She lives in the Pacific Northwest with her husband, three school-aged children, two spoiled Norwegian Elkhounds and cats who think they rule the house.

For more on Melissa's books, visit her website at www.melissamcclone.com.

Thank you for reading

The Cinderella Princess

If you enjoyed this book, you can find more from all our great authors at TulePublishing.com, or from your favorite online retailer.

TULE
PUBLISHING

Made in United States
Troutdale, OR
04/13/2024

19166243R00127